Silver Bullets

Laird Ryan States

Special Thanks to:

Gayleen Froese, as always
Tom Cantine and Anne Harwood, my editors
Meshon Cantrill for a last minute save
Eric Lindgren, for the logo
Quinn Kurenda, Steven Angel, Megan Cheesbrough, and Minister Faust
for support and assistance

And, especially to my father, John States, for liking westerns, even when I was
too dumb to get why.

CHAPTER ONE

Edmonton, Alberta 2008

WHAT IS OFFICIALLY KNOWN OF Arise-Ye-Sons-of-Israel Parker amounts to a handful of anecdotes handed down by word of mouth, recorded only occasionally in the history books. He was never immortalized by Ned Buntline and his ilk, never a dime novel celebrity. He never toured the eastern stages like Bill Cody or Bill Hickok. His death is not recorded, and so there is no ignominious shooting in the back as in the case of Jesse James. There is no hand of cards made famous and unlucky by the circumstance of his death. His only real claim to minor fame comes from his participation in the famous Gunfight at Clanton Stables. During that fight, it is said that he shot down six men. It is also said that he was himself shot twelve times but didn't fall until the shooting was finished. It's said that the local Indians nursed him back to health and he is supposed to have lived. His known story ends there, and many scholars have assumed the rumours of his recovery were exaggerated by the people of Clanton, who held him in high esteem.

There's no exaggeration, however, in the statement that Parker survived. If anything, it's a grotesque understatement. That gunfight took place in 1883, and Parker is still alive today. I am here, in fact, to meet with him, at the suggestion of one of his old acquaintances.

His house, in Edmonton Canada, is located in a neighbourhood called Alberta Avenue. It's north of the downtown core, filled with what passes for older homes in this much younger country. The houses date to the 1910's, old for the west, old for this city. The area has clearly seen better days. The main drags are frequented by prostitutes, vagrants, and the usual sorts of people that society leaves behind. Artists have settled in with them as well, as has been the custom since the beginning of cities. Sharing the neighbourhood as well are young families for whom the house prices here are, if not attractive, at least feasible in this boom-time oil-rich economy.

The area is said to be improving rapidly. I admit to nervousness in parking my rental car. Some blocks are better than others here. This one is not one of those. The houses are particularly frightening and shabby. Aside from his. It's tall and narrow, painted a pale blue. The slat fence seems to have been whitewashed recently. There's something slightly sinister about the pristine nature of this house in contrast to the rest of the block, something set apart.

I ring his doorbell. For a long awkward moment, I worry that he has forgotten I'm to come. There's no answer and no sound from inside. I stand in the autumn chill, my breath faintly visible. The air is full of the smells of fresh-fallen leaves, the slight tang of car exhaust. I turn to go, and then the door opens.

The man at the door is perhaps five-foot-three, Asian. He is dressed in a long white nightdress. He looks as if he might be a thousand years old. His face is, though I hate to say it, wizened. His bald head is spotted and the skin over it seems fish-scale-thin and pale.

"I'm looking for Harry Parker," I say, slowly. "Have I got the right place?"

The ancient man nods slowly and opens the front door, turning and walking inside. He says nothing as he shuffles back to the front room and sits himself back down in a large overstuffed chair of green leather. He pulls a coarse blanket up over his lap as though intending to nap.

The house smells of tobacco and strong liquor. There is a spittoon in the hall, and another in the front room near where the old man sits. The wood on the floors is oak, freshly waxed and shining. I feel as though I've stepped back in time. This is my grandmother's house before I was born. That's not actually correct. This is the house my grandfather might have kept had he lived as a bachelor. There are stacks of hardcover books and newspapers on the floor everywhere, the ashtrays full to bursting. Women rarely live like this. It's a sort of controlled squalor. And yet, for all of it, it seems to be very well-kept. The walls are painted, free of cracks.

It's September 15, 2008 today and, if Parker is really living here, he would be 167 years old.

I am about to ask the man in the chair if Parker is home. I'm interrupted when the man himself comes up the stairs. He looks at me from the other end of the hallway. I take a deep breath at the sight of him. He is five and a half feet tall, shorter than I would have expected. He has long ash blond hair, tied back with a shoelace into a long pony tail that hangs between his shoulder blades. His moustaches are long and a much lighter blond. His eyes are a deep and vibrant blue, and there is no trace of rheum to them. He wears jeans and leather boots and a blue cotton button down shirt with a western collar and a black string tie. He might be forty years old, or sixty. He has the sort of face that makes it hard to tell. No grey in his hair, no creeping hairline. No deep wrinkles or creases. He nods politely.

"Charley let you in?" he asks.

For a moment, I can only nod, as I put things together. The ancient Asian man who let me in is Indian Charley. Indian Charley was said to be Parker's best friend and boon companion. Also, he was supposed to be an Indian of the Ute tribe. He, at least, looked his age.

"Yes," I answer at last. "I'm Tom Bradstreet. I'd called ahead."

"Aw hell. That's right," he says, "You're the Irish writer come to talk to me about living forever. Sorry. I clean forgot."

He smiles broadly, and shakes his head slightly side to side as though ashamed. I feel my face responding with an unbidden smile of my own, and I offer him my hand to shake. He steps forward, wiping his palm on the front of his pants before clasping my hand. His grip is firm and cool and he makes eye contact as he shakes.

"I might have gussied up the place a bit had I remembered. I'm as easy to distract these days as a sailor in a French whorehouse. Can I get you something to cut the thirst? The wind out there is dry as hell this afternoon."

"I'm fine, thanks," I answer, and he smiles.

"Foyne," he says, mimicking me. "I love the way you Micks talk. Set a spell."

He moves me into the front room. I take a seat on a leather sofa, while he sits by the unlit brick fireplace on a simple and unadorned wooden chair. It looks out of place in the room.

"So," I say, "You're Arise-Ye-Sons-Of-Israel Parker?"

"I'd rather you called me Harry. Never did care for my full name much. You could break your teeth on that many hyphens."

"However you like," I say.

3

"You seem awfully quiet for an Irishman, no offense. Most of you fellers could talk a man to death, and there you sit, mouth clapped shut like a schoolmarm's knees at a social tea."

I find myself struggling for a handhold on this conversation. I'm a journalist. I was, anyway, and that's the way I approach practically every situation in my life. I want to remain objective, treat this like an interview. On the other hand, Harry and I have something in common with each other. We've both very much outlived our expiration dates.

"Is there any way you can verify that you are, in fact, Harry Parker?" I ask, trying to keep my detachment.

"I reckon there must be a dozen ways. Probably you could check the records on this house here. I ain't hardly tried to hide. Ain't hardly had to. You'd be surprised to see how hard the world works to explain away a two-hunnert-year-old man."

"Extraordinary claims require extraordinary proof," I start. He cuts me off.

"I got no desire to prove fuckin' anything to anyone. I am who I say I am, and you can believe it or don't as you choose. If the papers came round, I'd like as not deny it, just to avoid the trouble."

He's not even slightly angry. I'm not the first visitor to come to see him about this. It's part of his job, I've been told. He explains the rules for those of us who have somehow fallen off the pages of Death's accounting ledger, and lays down the law.

"Christ," I say, "Sorry. Rude. I invited myself here."

"Don't fuss me any, son. Took me years, most of 'em far from pretty before I really believed it myself, deep down in the bones. You'd be crazy as hell if you didn't have doubts of your own."

Charley lets loose a long sigh that rattles in his chest. I look at him with some concern and turn to Harry.

"Is he alright?"

"He'll be fine when he wants to get up," Harry says. "Whenever that turns out to be."

"He let me in just a minute ago," I say.

"Sleepwalking," Harry says. "You get used to it."

Harry crosses the floor with a grace that seems impossibly young and pulls the red and blue Indian blanket up tighter under Charley's chin, and he runs a hand over Charley's hair. "Rest up," Harry says to him with soft and genuine care, and sits back down.

"So," he says, "You're an immortal, then?"

I am silent for a moment, and then I clear my throat.

"I don't know that," I say. "All I know is that I've not aged a day since the eighties, and that I should have died from AIDS at least ten years ago. Now I don't have a trace of it in me."

"Sounds like immortality to me, son."

"That's the majority opinion among my friends, yeah."

"Who sent you to me?"

"Mr. Holmes," I answer.

"Still playing with his fuckin' bees?" he asks

"I believe so."

"Well, if he reckons you for the eternal, he's probably right. He's a stuck-up son of a bitch, but he don't miss much. Any idea how it happened?"

"Magic," I say, feeling, immediately, like a twat. "An old boyfriend of mine did something mad. He sacrificed his eyes and mind for it. Whatever it was, it must have worked."

"Well," he says, "that's a new one on me. Ain't never met one got the deal by witchin' before."

There's no reaction to me talking about magic, nor any snide judgment about finding out that I'm queer. I'm not sure which has me the most off-guard.

"Holmes told me I was an odd one. Of course, I thought that was stating the obvious, right?"

"Well, I've seen enough of life so far to know that I never know everything I fuckin' need to know, let alone what I want to know. Aside from the AIDS, you encountered any serious threats to life and limb?"

"I've twice cut my thumb to the bone slicing cheese and bread. Within a minute or so, I've been fine."

He nods.

"Sounds to me like however you got it, you've got the full package. You ever seen gutsilver?"

"I don't even know what that is."

"Ever bleed quicksilver?"

"No."

Harry reaches down and lifts his pant cuff. He pulls out a knife from his boot that is the size of my forearm and then slices his forearm. I wince, and he shows the wound to me. There is a thin line of red running down his arm, blood sliding down his forearm. A shimmering silver liquid slides out from deep inside the wound. It slips down and seems to grab at the trail of blood, pulling it back in slender ribbons that seep back through his skin, leaving his arm as smooth and unscarred as when he started. He puts the knife back where he found it.

"That's the usual for most of us. I call it gutsilver. Holmes calls it the Chalice. Some call it the Holy Mirror. All kinds of names for it, but it's what keeps me breathing and farting and cussing long past my natural time."

"Christ," I say. "That is the strangest thing I've ever seen."

"Life's long," he says, "Give her time."

"They call you the Sheriff," I say.

"I am that. I keep law for folks what don't die natural."

"Is that an elected position, then?" I ask.

"Kind of," he says with a wry grin.

"How's that?" I ask.

"I been elected on account of if you want to kill one of us, I'm the only one who can do it."

Thoughts of what it really means to live forever have haunted me for the last twenty years. I've considered the benefits and I've tried to make peace with the possibilities. I've also realized that where I once thought forward to my death and was met with a blank kind of dread and horror at the thought of my demise, I now find myself facing the equally horrible mystery of a life without end. There is another kind of horror in the thought of outliving the world I know. Can I adjust? Would I? I look at Harry and while I wouldn't look at him twice on the street, except to think him a little eccentric, talking to him is genuinely unsettling. He doesn't even try to sound current. Holmes, too, had seemed absolutely trapped in his Edwardian heyday. I'd thought it affectation, but I was no longer sure.

The feeling of the infinite stretching before me stopped. I was looking my death in his smiling face. If ever I needed to stop short my life, Harry Parker was the one to see. Apparently, the only one.

"The only one?" I repeat my thought aloud.

"Only one we know of. Reckon there must have been others. Reckon there'll be more sometime."

"I see." What else can I say? There's none of Holmes' talking around the issue with Harry. He talks plainly, likely takes pride in doing so.

"Now, who the hell knows. You might die in ways we mostly don't. You're an odd duck and all. So I don't know if anything I can tell you holds true in your particular case. Unless you're a vampire. From what you told me, you ain't. And if Holmes had sent me a vampire, he'd have more to worry about than you."

"Right," I say, pausing as I digest what he just told me "Anything you can tell me would be helpful, mind. I've only just started to admit I've got a problem, and I'm willing to learn. I'd love some answers."

"Leastways you got the sense to see it as a problem," he says leaning back, tipping the front two legs of his chair up off the floor.

"Anything you don't understand and can't change is probably trouble," I say.

He laughs.

"I'll tell you what I know," he says. "But talking is thirsty work, and I'm drinking whiskey. You sure I can't get you one?"

"Thanks, no," I say. "I quit drinking. Goes badly for the men in my family."

"Suit yourself," he says as he walks into the kitchen attached to the front room by way of the dining room. He comes back in with a bottle and a glass and pours himself one. "For my own part, life's too fucking long to face it sober."

CHAPTER TWO

Sill Creek, Ohio 1867

ARISE SAT ON THE BANKS of the creek. He was dressed in simple black trousers and a white buttoned shirt. His hair was bleached nearly white by the summer sun. He had sprouted recently and his pants were too short for him now. A full inch of bare skin showed between cuff and sock. He could no longer button the cuffs on his sleeves, so he wore them rolled to halfway up the forearm. That looked less ridiculous.

Laying beside him on the grass was a little green rucksack that he had found by the side of the road. His mother had patched the ragged hole with a piece of flour sack. It pretty much went everywhere that he did. It was full of tiny scraps of paper that he salvaged from here and there. These were covered with poems. He had one of these scraps on his lap, and a pencil in his hand. He was trying to find words that played well together. Poetry was his Concern. Sometimes God spoke through him. Sometimes he found the words on his own. Some days, he just had to wrestle them onto paper. This was one of those days.

Birdsong echoed off the water. He leaned back his head and smiled, closing his eyes, feeling sun and wind on his face. He smelled the faint scent of fresh bread wafting from some distant sill. Somewhere back behind him, he heard church letting out. He heard people talking and little kids running around like fools giggling. It was a beautiful day. He expected that, soon enough, the banks of the creek would be full of people with packed lunches. That was fine, and even better than fine, but it wasn't conducive to the work of poetry.

Arise didn't have many friends in Sill Creek. He and his folks were the only Friends in town. The people in Sill Creek were polite and kind to him and his family for the most part, but they called them Quakers behind their backs, as though it were some sort of a bad word or as though it would offend. His family did not attend the church services either. This set them apart, set the occasional tongue to wag, the odd hen to cluck behind her wing.

Back home in Pennsylvania, there had been a congregation of Friends. He remembered their monthly meetings with a warm fondness. The chairs were set out to face each other in an open circle. They had all sat together waiting for God to speak through them. Sometimes, they would sit in silence for the hour, but sometimes someone would speak and they would all discuss God's message. After the meetings, everyone would talk and laugh and the children would play. He hadn't played very much since they'd moved. Now he was too old for that, and he'd found his Concern anyway.

Thinking about that time and place was something he tried not to do. Remembering Pennsylvania darkened his thoughts nearly to pure black if he did it for long. He started to compare his neighbours here to the Friends left behind. When he did that, he couldn't help but feel a sense of loss and a dim anger at the new folks for not meeting that level. He was then angry at himself for judging, and for not having made enough of an effort to make new friends here. They'd been here seven years now, and he had to recognize that some of the distance was kept by him. Most of all, he was forced to think about Johnny.

Johnny had been born seven minutes after he had. If he'd been born first, Johnny would have been saddled with the ridiculous puritan name passed down through his family. Instead, he'd waited patiently for his brasher brother to elbow his way out first. That had set the tone for them. Though they looked as alike as any two children ever had, they were different of soul. Johnny had been nearly silent while Arise chattered. Johnny was introspective and gentle. Arise had been rough and tumble. This seemed to delight his parents, who saw in their relationship balance and support and compromise. Certainly, he had loved his brother with a depth of feeling he'd not known since, and which he felt unlikely to know ever again. Having Johnny around meant there was no such thing as loneliness, nor did he ever feel less than understood.

Johnny had died in such a reasonless and capricious way that Arise had almost lost his faith. He had been waiting for Arise out front of the feed store, standing next to a loaded cart. With no warning, the hitch gave way and the cart tipped back. Johnny had been crushed under the cart as it rolled and left him buried under bloody hay. Arise had heard the sounds of the crunching wood, and the abbreviated sudden squeal from his brother. The shopkeeper had kept him from going outside while the other men rushed. He imagined it was meant as a kindness. When he was finally released, the bloody hay left behind in the street forced him to imagine what had happened, and how bad it had been. He had a powerful imagination.

They moved away soon after that. The place was too full of sad reminders. It was too easy to be angry at Henry Lee who had owned the cart, even though they knew full well it was pure accident. The first year was the worst. Sadness had marooned them all on a sort of desert island, bereft of human contact. He had no idea how his father had managed to keep to his chores, but the fact that he could was what kept Arise working at his side. There was always work, and crops did not wait.

The saddest lesson for him had been his own recovery from grief. When you lost a twin, it was supposed to be like a piece of you had died. No piece of him had. He was wounded, surely, but not killed. He had ached with loss and, so many times, had turned to the empty bed as if to speak, and then burst into tears. He sometimes wished he had died. He hadn't. His life went on, a little less filled up with joy. He had learned there was no loss that truly would steal his ability to go on. He'd felt, at first, a sense that he was committing an act of betrayal by ceasing to weep.He'd been changed. The brashness of him had worn smoother; a combination of sadness and the unfamiliarity of new surroundings had turned him within. He'd become more like his brother and made peace with that. Part of how he healed was to carry his brother's spirit within him.

This was, he supposed, not the worst way to make your peace with the death of someone you loved. It didn't leave him any more at peace with a world where a seven-year-old boy died for no reason at all.

He rubbed his eyes and shook his head, trying to shake off thoughts the way a cow brushed away flies with its tail. He tucked his papers into his rucksack and the pencil back behind his ear. He'd known he'd at have to find some place else to write today once church let out. Besides, lunch was probably nearly ready at home, and he was hungry. There were likely some chores needed doing as well.

He headed along the banks of the creek to the road, running into one or two people and smiling at them politely. He was glad that he had not taken his hat. That prevented the awkwardness of having not to remove it whenever he passed a lady. The Friends had strict rules against that. It implied some people worthy of more respect than others. It was one of those rules he thought was sort of silly, but the last time he'd taken off his hat for a girl, his father had given him a stern talk. It wasn't worth the fuss.

The sun was hot enough that the back of his shirt was damp and starting to stick to him. It wasn't a long walk from town to his father's farm, but it was long enough that he wished he had a canteen with him.

As he came to the lane that led down to his house, he heard a rustling in the trees that lined it. He smiled, and turned to the noise.

"Gus, you'd make a lousy Indian," he said.

Gus Walker lurched out from cover. He was seventeen, and taller than any man in town, even hunched over as he was. Tall as he was, he wasn't built for it. His chest was sunken, and too narrow and his jaw was long. His hair was black, his eyes brown. People in town had sometimes whispered that he looked half-Indian. Arise was pretty sure that they were wrong. Gus' pa wasn't the sort of man who was likely to have let his wife get away with that kind of a thing. He was a drinking man, and free with his fists and his belt. Gus' ma was from Mexico, and if there was Indian in the family, it probably came from somewhere back in her family tree. People loved to gossip, and they loved to whisper about people.

"I wasn't hiding, anyhow," Gus said, with a look of indifference. "Just coming back from church?"

Arise looked at him with no expression.

"Sure was. You?"

"Yep. I was there singing hymns all morning to beat the band. Surprised you didn't hear me."

"I'm more surprised you beat me back here at the pace you limp around."

Gus pushed a lick of hair back off his face, and considered thoughtfully.

"Least I'm not a Quaker."

"Naw," Arise said, "You're just a regular sinner."

They laughed, and walked together toward the house. Arise still thought he could smell fresh bread. Unless the wind were stronger than it clearly was, or unless he was a dog, he was pretty sure he was more wishing for it than smelling it.

"You hungry?" he said to Gus. "You know you're always welcome."

"I ate already, thanks."

Gus rarely ate, and often said he had just to avoid the opportunity. For awhile, Arise had taken it for pride, or for some kind of shame. He knew better now. Gus was just one of those people that never got hungry. He seemed to resent food, and the need to eat, as some kind of a chore. It was beyond Arise to fully understand.

"Well, what does bring you around then?" Arise asked.

"Probably here to court after your ma."

Arise punched him in the arm.

"Don't get salty on a Sunday."

Gus laughed.

"Hell, I'd get salty with her on a Sunday if I could. I'd get salty with her any day of the week that "ends in a 'y'.""

"You're a wicked sinner, Walker."

"Well, life's short, my friend."

"Hell goes on for a spell, though."

Gus waved his hands in front of him, and shook his head.

"Peh. Let's just agree to disagree on that point. I ain't fussed about hell."

Arise held his tongue, and patted his friend on the back. There was no sense arguing with a good man over a difference of theology.

"Fair enough."

"Hey, Harry," Gus said, "you in a particular hurry to get home?"

Arise recognized a tone in his friend's voice that caused him concern. Something had Gus astir. He wanted to talk, but he was too slick and tough to say so. Arise swallowed back the imagined smell of the bread.

"Not a particular hurry no. Why's that?"

"I got something I want you to see."

"All right, what is it?" Arise said, stopping to look Gus in the eyes.

"Just come and see."

Arise shrugged, and they turned and walked over to the gap in the trees that Gus had laid wait in. The two of them had long since walked a trail clear between their farms. They went on in a companionable silence, which was one of the things he liked about Gus. Gus didn't feel the need to talk all the time. He picked his words. It appealed to the poet side of Arise, but also made him feel safe. He had to slow his pace because, even with his added height, Gus moved slowly. Arise had gotten good at making the pace look natural, so as not to shame him.

In a few minutes they came to the grazing pasture and the cattle looked up for a moment, half interested, and went back to their chewing. Gus led them off to the north corner, which felt like habit. There was a little clump of trees there that they had used as a hideaway from adults for as long as they'd been friends.

In the shade, he felt a lot cooler and more relaxed and easy. He lay on the hard packed dirt, using his rucksack and his poems as a pillow.

"Ah," he said, "see, this is nice, this moment, just now."

"Sure is. Wait here."

Gus moved over into the trees and dropped to his knees, rummaging. He came back with a blue handkerchief wrapping something. He put it in Arise's hands. It was heavy and hard. He felt his stomach roll, pretty sure what it was. To be certain, he lifted the handkerchief free. It was an old revolver. He had never seen one before. It was the single most beautiful thing he'd ever held. He turned it over in his hands.

"That," Gus said, "is a Colt revolver."

"What the hell are you doing with a gun?" Arise asked, lowering his voice midway through the question.

"Found it up the creek a bit. It was rusted half to hell, but I cleaned it up some. I expect someone is missing it, or ain't able to."

"Take this thing away from me. Friends don't carry guns. It'd break my mother's heart if she even saw me holding one."

Arise didn't hand it back to him, and Gus didn't move to take it. He just stood there with a grin.

"So hand it back to me, then," Gus said.

Arise couldn't stop looking at the pistol, and then he looked up at Gus.

"Where's the trigger?" Arise asked, puzzled, as he'd expected to see one.

Gus looked excited.

"Point the business end over there and cock the hammer at the back," Gus told him.

He raised the gun, pointing it into the distance. With his other hand, he pulled the hammer back until it caught. The trigger came out of a little recession just under the barrel, shiny and silver and deadly. If he chose to, he realized, he could point this gun at anyone, even Gus. Just pulling that tiny half moon of metal back would end that person forever. His stomach rolled, and he nearly dropped the thing.

"How...how do I uncock this thing?"

"Well," Gus said, "You can fire it. That'd do it. Or you can just slide the hammer back a little further and ease it slowly back in. Slowly, or you'll set off the cap just the same."

Arise handed Gus the gun in shaking hands, not trusting himself to do it, and not wanting to fire it off. Gus had no such caution. He pulled the trigger, blasting a hunk of bark off of one of the trees. Cattle spooked and birds flew. The noise was loud, just as loud as his father's old hunting musket, it seemed, but the gun was so much smaller that it seemed twice as terrible. Gus laughed like a little kid and tucked the gun in the back of his pants, looking at him with wide, happy eyes.

"Gus," Arise said, "does anyone else know you have that thing?"

"Hell no, Harry, and we ain't telling them neither. This gun is my ticket to the whole world. I'm gonna head out west, and make a name for myself somewhere, and she's coming with me. Keep me safe, and keep me employed."

"You're out of your fool mind," Arise said.

"Hell I am! This chest of mine runs in the family, and my grandpa didn't live to see forty. Most men in my family don't. You think I want to live my whole life and then die in this little mudhole? Out west a man good with a gun can earn his keep with it, and live a life with some spice to it."

"Yeah, or he can take a bullet to the heart and die before he's twenty, just the same."

Gus shrugged. "Beats dying slow."

"I believe in peace, Gus. That gun is everything wrong with the world wrapped up in a pretty package. Let's go together, right now, and throw it in the creek where it can't hurt anybody, especially you."

"I know you Quakers hold to peace, and that's just fine for you. I don't have any pressing desire to shoot a man neither, as it happens. But a man with a gun is a world safer than a man without. If this were a world full of Quakers, I'm sure we'd be happier, and I'm sure you'd be right. It ain't, however, full of Quakers. It's a world chock full of sons of bitches loaded for bear."

"And you feel the need to bolster their fuckin' numbers?"

Gus reacted like he'd been slapped. In seven years, Arise had sworn twice in front of him. Once when he'd put a potato fork through his own foot, and just then.

"The world is what it is, Harry, not what we wish it was."

"So you just give up and give in, then?" Arise said, gritting his teeth and narrowing his eyes.

"I ain't giving up, I'm joining up, dammit. I want to join the world."

"If you believe that peace is right, but you take up arms, then you are a coward."

"Maybe so, Harry. But I'm a coward with a gun."

"My name is Arise."

"Yeah, I know that," Gus said. "I reckon, though, that I'll keep to calling you Harry, so as I don't bust out laughing."

Arise felt a fist clench at his side. He really wanted to haul off and plant that fist between the eyes of his friend, but he kept his temper in check.

"Do what you will," Arise said, getting to his feet.

"C'mon," Gus said, "don't walk away feeling raw."

Arise drew in a long breath and let it out.

"Gus," he said, "you have been my only friend since I moved here. If you leave town with that gun, you'll go by yourself. That'll pain me more than a little because you've come to be like a brother to me. I'd rather you didn't go but, if you feel that God is moving you on that path, then you will have to take it. I know it isn't mine."

Gus looked at him and they were quiet.

"You're a loyal friend to me, Harry."

"You can count on that, Gus Walker. Even if you go."

They shook hands with a solemnity that seemed older than the two of them.

Arise turned to head back to his father's house, and then turned his head half-way back, not looking at Gus.

"You let me know before you do light out," he said, and kept walking as Gus sat in the dirt, gun in hand, considering his future.

CHAPTER THREE

The West, a long time ago

THEY TOLD XIAO LE HE was born on the moon. He had fallen from the sky as a child, so long ago that he barely remembered it. No matter how hard he tried, he could not remember his own people, or how he had come to fall from the moon. He could only remember being found. Even that was a memory of a memory, as hazy as a reflection in a running stream

The night he arrived, the People had made their camp and most were asleep when a sound like thunder rang. A bright light streaked across the sky. It was so large and so bright that you could hold up both hands and not cover it up. The thing in the sky had broken in two smaller pieces. One kept west across the sky, until it went out of sight. The much smaller piece seemed to drop straight down, glowing like a falling ember, a spark.

Two scouts ran to see the place where it fell, and, after many hours, found it. There was a man-sized piece of grey stone cracked open like an egg. The inside of that egg was lined in soft red cloth. The stone was warm to the touch, and touching it made the tiny hairs on their arms stand straight up. As the scouts were about to ask each other what to do, Xiao Le had stumbled back to the stone from the woods nearby. He looked to be four or five summers old. He wore a long green robe that fastened along the back with a series of opalescent buttons and cloth loops. His head was bald and smooth.

Back then he did not speak the language of the people, and the scouts tried to use sign language with him. All that he was able to communicate was his own name. Xiao Le. He had been called that through his childhood. They had taken him into the tribe. His new parents had lost a son to sickness, and were only too happy to take him as their own.

It was always known that he would one day become a great man. There was no question about his destiny. Clearly, he had been sent to them for some reason. With that in mind, it would have been very easy for him to have become lazy or arrogant. It's to the great credit of the People that they did not let this happen. Though he had come to them in such a strange way and, though he was obviously bound for something of massive import, they never lost sight of the fact that he was just a boy. They never let him forget his own fallibility. Gentle mockery can be worth more to a young boy than any stern talk.

Though he was different in appearance, his skin pale and wan compared to their coppery tones, his eyes at a slight angle and with a crease, once his hair had grown in he was able to fit in without constantly being reminded that he was from some other place.

For his first few years, he would sometimes lapse into the language he had spoken before, but now, on the cusp of manhood, he struggled to remember any of it. He hadn't spoken it, except in his sleep, in years. He supposed that was only natural.

He was, at this moment, walking through the woods looking for his name. Now that he was to be a man, he needed his adult name. He had eaten the roots and mushrooms given to him, fought to keep from sicking them up after, and was sent on his naming quest alone. This was a stronger drug than any he had known. Sweat beaded on his forehead, even though the night was cool, and he was not tired. He was dizzy and his arms and legs felt strange and light.

He walked with a slow deliberate pace, waiting for a spirit guide to reveal itself. He came to a spot where the trees crowned. Through them he saw a circle of inky sky, stars, and the moon, full and bright. As always, the sight of it made his heart ache for a home he had never known. The medicine and the night had pulled him in. He could not look away. The surface of the moon shimmered and pulsed in time with his heartbeat.

Something struck him between the shoulder blades and he fell forward, gasping. He rolled over and saw the bear arched up on hind legs and about to slam the full weight of its body down onto him. He should have been terrified. He had somehow wandered blindly into the path of this mother bear. He could see her teats swollen, and knew that cubs must be near. The moment dragged on, and though he knew he was going to die, his only question, his only actual thought, was wondering how this death fulfilled his destiny. He almost wanted to laugh. There was no fear, no anger at the bear. It was humbling and hilarious. He closed his eyes and waited for her to land.

Instead, his ears nearly burst at the sound of thunder. He felt the hair on his legs stand up, and then crisp and smoke. The flash of light was so bright that even after he opened his eyes, all he could see for several seconds were bright splotches, as though he'd stared at the sun. He could smell burning fur. He heard the bear screaming in pain. He blinked furiously and saw the scorch on the earth at his feet. He looked up and saw her running off in the clearing. The thick grease on her coat was still burning brightly, smoke trailing behind her as she ran blindly from the pain.

He could only hear his own breathing, once the sounds of the bear faded. He was alive, though he had no idea how or why. He stood up shakily, and reached back a hand. He felt blood where the bear had clawed at him, but there was no pain, and the blood was already sticky and half dried.

He looked up from his hand, and standing in front of him was a dark hole where a man should have been. He could see that it was smiling, but he could not have explained how. It looked as though a shadow had stood straight up off of the ground, but this shadow had weight. There was grass bent under where it stood.

The shadow put a hand on his shoulder. It made his skin tingle and he could hear a faint hum. The shadow smelled like the night after it rains.

"Xiao Le." The shadow spoke in the language of the People. "Tell them that I sent the lightning to save you."

"Who are you?" Xiao Le asked, shaking, still half sick from the medicine, and now from his own fear at coming so close to death.

"I don't know. I have never known."

The shadow stepped back, and the light faded through him slowly and softly until the shadow itself was gone and Xiao Le was alone.

This was the day that Xiao Le became Bear-On-Fire to his people, and to himself. There was too much power in the moment for him to be called anything else.

CHAPTER FOUR

Sill Creek, Ohio 1867-68

AS WAS THE CASE FOR most things with Gus, his obsession with the pistol had lasted about a week. He had not mustered up the gumption to light out west in the last two months, and had only occasionally gone on a tear about how, soon, he'd make his fortune on the frontier. Arise was glad of it. His own father had spent some time assisting in field hospitals during the War, one way a Friend could serve. Arise had sometimes asked to be told what it was like. His father had always answered that he was too young, and that war was too terrible a thing for a child to bear.

On the other hand, it seemed that some of the light had left Gus' eyes. Arise had the faint feeling that he had robbed Gus of his only dream, maybe even his Concern in this life. This was ridiculous, and he knew it. A person could not be kept from their Concern. If Gus could be persuaded to stay, then he probably had been meant to. Still, he felt that little nag that his words had somehow wounded a friend.

It was a cold late fall, frost coming at night, with winds that kept up all through the day. He was glad that harvest was over, and that winter was on the way. Winter was his favourite season. He loved the deep, calm snow that covered everything over and days spent by the fire, once the animals had been tended to. He didn't even mind chopping and fetching wood. In the winter, everything seemed to slow down. He was acutely aware of the bone-deep hatred most people had for the season, but for him it was like wrapping up in a deep quilt and simply feeling safe.

He had not laid a word on paper in two months, which was common for harvest. You made up for any rest in winter by the hard work of the fall. He was looking forward to a long season of trying to describe the world in ways nobody else had found. That was not an easy thing, but he was determined to do his best.

His father was reading from the family Bible in one chair, and he sat in another, thinking of how to start. His mother was in the kitchen, peeling potatoes for supper. There was going to be no shortage of potato in his diet this winter, he was sure. He was thankful that he was built to like them just fine.

Someone knocked at the door, and his mother asked him to answer it. He frowned, set down his work, and walked to the door. He opened it a crack. Gus was on the steps, the collar of his dark, woollen coat turned up against his neck. His face was pale, but blotched with spots of high, uneven colour. His cheeks were wet.

"Gus? Are you feeling all right?"

"Is your pa at home, Harry?"

Arise's mother saw the look on Gus' face and set down her work, coming to the door and coming over to them.

"Gus, what's happened?" she said.

"Hello, Mrs. Parker. Is Mr. Parker at home?"

By that time, his father was already at the door, his face calm but concerned. He was a tall, strong man. Arise and Francis Parker looked nearly comical side by side as father and son.

"What can I help you with, son?" Francis said.

"My ma asked me to fetch you. We need your help to move Pa. He died, sir."

There was a moment of silence and each of his parents, in unison, put a hand on Arise's shoulders and squeezed.

"I'll get my coat," Francis said and went to the little closet near the door.

Arise stood still, looking at his friend. Gus was staring like a face in a painting, slow and calm, but behind his eyes there was a caged rat trying to claw its way out. Arise felt hot tears come to his eyes, trying to fight them back. His mother wept with no shame as she transferred the potatoes to a pot of water to keep them from rust.

The four of them walked the quarter-mile in silence. Arise, not knowing what to say, said nothing. His parents were quiet people, and had learned that sometimes words, for all their considerable power, made for nothing

The front door was open when they got there. Gus' mother was on her knees, on the front stoop, wailing and pulling out handfuls of her dark hair, peppered with grey. Gus' brother and sister stood in the porch, eyes wide and still. Arise's mother knelt beside the grieving widow and gently eased her back into the house, whispering and stroking her hair and closing the door to keep the heat in.

Gus' father was facing up, his tin coffee cup still in his hand, coffee soaking into quilted rug and in a puddle on the plank floor. He was a big man, tall and fat, weighing over 300 pounds. His eyes were open, but rolled back so they were mostly white. The right side of his face looked like a candle someone had let melt in the sun, drooped and flaccid. The other half had pulled tight, or looked that way in comparison. The sight of him brought a sour vomitous taste to the back of Arise's throat. Francis Parker placed his coat over the man's face.

"Arise, take his ankles, son."

Doing as he was told by automatic response, he picked up the man's legs. They were still warm, but they were not as warm as they should have been. It was such a small thing but it made all the difference in the world. This wasn't a person anymore. Whatever angry soul had once been here in this body, it was long gone now.

They carried him to the bedroom, with great difficulty, and laid him on the sheets. They crossed his arms over his chest. Gus stood by them.

"Thank you," Gus said. "I couldn't lift him."

"No man should have to lift his own father," Francis said, and put a hand on Gus' shoulder. Gus buried his face down on Francis' shoulder, bending to do it, and sobbed. Arise had never seen Gus experience something so profound as this emotion, but he could empathize. He remembered the tears the day his brother was put in the ground. He remembered his father crying for Johnny with just the same strength.

Arise's mother was on her hands and knees in the kitchen, wiping up the spills of both coffee and urine. Gus' father had wet himself as he went down. Arise hadn't noticed until they set him on the bed. He pulled a blanket up over the man as Gus cried. Neither he nor Gus were much consoled.

Arise could hear his friend sobbing, and the widow in her kitchen wailing, her younger children sobbing beside her. There was no poetry in this. No poetry could make this less sad, nor even describe the pain, the ugliness with which people left the world.

His father had taught him that the flesh was like an envelope, and once the soul was free, there was no more use for it than for an envelope when the letter was read. What his father never took into account was that a used envelope was like gold to Arise. It was a place to leave poems.

What use was there in the flesh, then? Was it of less use than an envelope? It seemed a terrible waste, and a cruel one, that a human being left behind such a mess when it died.

The next day, the town helped to bury Gus' father. There was a service in the town church. Out of respect, he and his parents attended. He did not feel the presence of God there. He wondered, angrily, if the omnipresence of God were a myth. Perhaps God lived only in Pennsylvania. Certainly, Arise had seen no sign of Him since the move.

And precious little before.

To have these thoughts in a church pained him. It pained him more to hear his best friend choke through a eulogy for his own father and to note, first and foremost, the artlessness of it. He realized that he could have written a better eulogy for the man himself, even though he had never liked him. He had been cruel and nasty, and all of Arise's prayers for him to treat his family with more kindness had gone unanswered. Unless one considered this as the answer to his prayer.

His cheeks flushed with shame at his own sins of pride, his blasphemies against the good intentions of God. He shut his eyes tight and prayed an apology to God, and asked for strength enough to bear this pain, and to help his friend.

For the next few months he spent as much time at their house as he did his own. He helped Gus with chores, and with the chopping of wood, and helped him to prepare for the spring planting. Gus was now responsible for feeding his family. Whatever hopes he'd had for running off and living his dreams were as dead as his father.

Just like that, Gus died while Arise watched, slowly, as the winter went on. As the realization dawned exactly what he was responsible for, and the shape of his life to come, it put the light out in his eyes the rest of the way. He walked, and talked, and even cracked the occasional joke, but it was not that Gus had changed, or smoothed as he himself had when he lost his twin. Gus was just a shell now. The soul had left the envelope, and this envelope was only useful for farming and feeding a family. It had no other interests, and no other purpose.

Arise lay in his bed. The spring thaw was starting to loosen the earth after the worst winter of his life. He hadn't written a poem since before harvest, and didn't know if he ever would again. What use did a man like

Gus have for a poem, and all the thousands of men in his situation? If something happened, God forbid, to his own father, what would happen to him? Would he become what amounted to a beast of burden himself. Would he give up his own concern as quickly, as thoroughly as Gus had been forced by love for his family to do? He couldn't even find ways to consider the thought, to understand or express it. It seemed to him that words didn't have the strength to really express these feelings, and if they couldn't do that, what was the point of them.

Absent poetry, he had no purpose of his own, and was now certain that he could never carry on with farming as his father had done. He wished he had stayed in school, that he was the sort of person that could travel the world and see the halls of learning. There was no more profit in that line of thought than there was in wishing he could fly. Neither was going to happen, and he'd look like a fool doing either one.

Feeling no small amount of shame, he snuck out of the house in the early morning. He wrote a note to his mother and father which simply said that he was sorry, but that he'd been called by God to head west. He promised to try to wire back money to pay for the horse he was taking.

He saddled up the old girl, and rode out across the fields to the little clump of trees where he and Gus had hidden together and shared all their secrets. He found the hole that they had lined with oiled canvas and then covered with a rock. All manner of things were in that hole. Among the penny candy and half-smoked cigars he found the gun. He could see that four barrels were still loaded, though probably not to be relied on if he understood how they worked. It was better than nothing if he was taking to the open road.

His pack was full of potatoes, and some bread, and jars of jam. He had about a half a dollar saved up. He had a gun, and he had the strong need to head west.

He saw it this way: he and Gus, they'd each had a dream. Gus had wanted the west, and the rough life. Arise had wanted to be a poet. Gus had no further use for dreams, now. If Arise'd been less good with words, he might have failed to talk Gus out of leaving. He felt like he'd done Gus a fatal injury to the soul. With words. Fuck words forever.

Watching Gus lose his dream, Arise had managed to misplace his own as well. He was sure that Gus wouldn't mind lending his. Worse, he was sure that Gus would never so much as notice.

It was a perfectly good dream, basically as long as you didn't believe in God anymore. He went ahead, stopped believing, and ran away from farms and families forever.

CHAPTER FIVE

Arizona 1871

BEAR-ON-FIRE WAS WANDERING again, as he had done, off and on, for more than a hundred summers since his naming. He could not stay with the People. His timelessness provoked fear and jealousy. His strength had intensified with age, to the point that he was afraid to touch normal people. His casual walking speed was such that he could cover vast stretches of area without tiring. He could see farther than the hawk and hear two blades of grass rubbing together. He was as powerful and as dangerous a creature as the world had ever seen. He could not die.

Men had tried, both white and red, to kill him. He had been shot at many times, and each time it had hurt badly, but each wound had healed up almost as soon as the blood started to flow. His blood was laced with some sky metal that shone like a white man's mirror, but which flowed like water. Where it passed, it was as though time itself was turned back. Wounds vanished.

Sometimes he felt it moving in him, changing the nature of what made up his body and turning his muscle and his bone into some new thing. For a long time, that had scared him. He had wondered what he was turning into. After a hundred years, he had determined that what he was turning into was just a better and stronger version of himself, and stopped worrying

It had also made him feel a terrible solitude. He did not stay in one place for any longer than a few days. He did not make friends. He often felt he should intervene in one situation or another. He knew that one such as he could change the course of a war, that he could turn the tide of many things. He did not feel his understanding of any situation was complete enough to act. He did not want to make any situation worse than it was.

From time to time, he would bring food to starving wagon trains caught up in winter storms. He had several times saved the life of someone threatened by robbers. He had rescued a number of wronged men from lynchings. He was able to do these things with a certainty he was doing good, and with the anonymity of a ghost, moving as swiftly as a strong wind.

He had fallen from the sky and was most probably a god of some kind. He would go about the earth doing the good works of a god. Once in a long while, he would see a man or a woman at a distance and he could tell by looking at them that they too had the sky metal flowing through them.

Once he had tried to approach one of these men. The man had fled by leaping away into the sky. Bear-on-Fire had watched him leap off into the distance in a series of jumps that took him a mile at a time.

Since then, he had simply nodded at a respectful distance, and the other party seemed surprised, but had not bolted away. He had taken this to mean that his kind, whatever they were, were solitary creatures. He did not mind.

He was sitting on the sand, next to the low-lying scrub, wiping his forehead with the sleeve of his white cotton shirt. The heat still made him thirst, and made him sweat. Neither of them bothered him so much that he could not appreciate the feel of the sun beating down on him, and reflecting back up at him from the sandy ground. He smiled at the sun.

He was watching a small group of the People as they walked under this heat. There were twelve of them counting children. They were not of the tribe who raised him, and they seemed accustomed to the heat and dust. The clothing they wore was light in colour, and minimal, the women and men both naked to the waist. The women were each carrying a baby in a light sling that cradled the child near her breast. One of the men was carrying a rifle. They had two horses heavy-laden with their provisions.

A boy of ten summers or so was impatient with the pace, and would run ahead, and circle back over and over. One of the older men clobbered him half-heartedly on the side of the head as he made his most recent turn, and the boy fell over laughing. He got up, and the man, his father or an uncle, Bear-On-Fire assumed, spoke to him. He could not quite understand what the man had said, but the boy started trudging along beside him in a sullen and exaggerated display of compliance. Bear-on-Fire laughed, and his laugh was loud enough that it was heard by them even though he was farther away than any of them could have ever seen. The party of travellers froze where they stood and the men looked carefully around themselves. He did not blame them, for this passage was known to be dangerous. A group of men had set themselves up nearby to prey on travellers, most especially coaches carrying mail and payroll. He felt badly that he'd scared them but, on the other hand, perhaps it taught them caution.

Two white men on horseback were hiding just up the trail from the People. He was waiting to see what would happen. These men made their living by stealing. Mostly they stole from the white man's government, the enemy of his people. He did not feel justified in taking the bread from their mouths. However, they sometimes robbed simple travellers passing through. He had seen them rob other white men, but they had killed nobody. They had left them with supplies and sent them on their way. This was dangerous, but not as dangerous as hanging for the murder of a white man.

White men did not often hang for murdering the People. He doubted these People had any valuable items except for the rifle, and their horses. They needed those to travel, to stay alive. It was an easy temptation for the white men to slaughter them for it. Many men would. Bear-On-Fire could not act until he knew.

He drew closer, staying as out of sight as best he could while still being able to intervene if he needed to.

The party came to the pass, and the white men rode out to stop them. There were two of them. One of them was an older man with a paunch, his hairline half-receded. His white undershirt was soaked with sweat and tobacco juice. He wore a round-topped hat with a narrow brim, and spat a fresh spray of tobacco into the sand as he levelled a shotgun at the travellers. His partner was much younger, barely a man at all. He was blond. His skin was burned, and he wore a hat similar to his older friend, only in worse repair. He was clean, but dusty, with blond moustaches. He had a revolver in his hand.

The traveler dropped his rifle, and the fat man turned to his younger partner.

"Lookit that," he said. "Goddamn, these Indians are stupid. Don't they know we're gonna kill them?"

"We ain't," said the other man, and his partner laughed.

"Fuck not?" he said, as the travellers tried to understand the English being spoken back and forth. Bear-on-Fire had learned English long ago. He'd realized he would have to.

"These people ain't got shit on them but food and shelter, Brett. We don't need either, and we don't kill for fuckin' sport."

"Maybe you don't."

Brett made as if to aim the gun and fire but, before he could even touch the trigger, the side of his head exploded with gore. The horses startled, and Brett hit the ground. The younger man had drawn his gun with a speed that was impressive. His eyes were wide with horror at what he'd done. He holstered his gun, and got off his horse.

The traveler picked up his gun and levelled it at the blond. The young man raised his hands and spoke to them in halting, cautious words of their own language. He could not understand all of their talk, but the young white man spoke slowly enough to follow. He told the People to keep on traveling, and that more of their kind were ahead and not far. He drew a crude map in the dirt with one finger, and talked with them for awhile. One of the women embraced him.

His name was Harry Parker. He asked them never to tell anyone what he'd done. They promised. He asked for water, and they gave him some.

The People went on their way, and Harry rode away in the direction they had come from. It was not the way back to his camp, but he could not go there. Bear-on-Fire watched him go as long as he could, but he needed to watch over his people here.

CHAPTER SIX

Clanton, Colorado 1880

HARRY PARKER WAS ALONE IN the saloon, long past closing. He had an arrangement with the owner, and a tab. He was drinking hard and leaning over a piece of paper with a pencil. His hat was on the seat beside him, and his brow was furrowed. There was a lantern turned up bright. It was his sole companion. He muttered half a verse under his breath. None of the locals were crazy enough to come into the place at this time of night. Even the reckless ones would have reconsidered once they saw the glass of whiskey beside him. Harry fancied a local brand called Panther Piss. It was cheap and nasty. When Harry drank it, which was often, he turned from a well-intentioned if rough-hewn man to a raving monster.

He was the law here, having retired, they said, from a life of robbing coaches and the occasional train. He'd been canny enough never to stand before a judge, so there was no impediment to him holding the position of Town Marshall. He did a fine job in keeping the general order so long as he was sober. When he was drunk, he seemed only to take it out on the sort of men who could usually do with a sound beating.

That night, there had been some famous English dandy in town, on a pleasure tour of America. Somehow he'd found his way to Clanton. He'd spoken before an audience of what passed for the educated in this piss-hole of a town, answering questions about England. They had held a supper and a dance in his honour in the town square, and once it got late, things wound down peaceably.

The dandy's coach was scheduled to leave at four in the morning, and he felt obligated to stay awake to make sure that it departed unmolested. He had a star on his chest, now, and that meant something.

He swallowed another slug of Panther Piss, and went to the keg to fill it again, making a notch in chalk on the side for Ronnie, the barkeep. He turned to go back to his scribbling, and was surprised to see the dandy standing there. It must have shown on his face.

"I beg your pardon," the dandy said, "but I just could not get a bit of sleep. I saw the light, and thought I might have a dram."

Harry shrugged.

"Why not? If you and your delicate constitution can find something behind that bar that suits you, then drink. By all means. I'll even buy."

The dandy smiled, his teeth wide and even.

"Is the keeper of the house not present?" the dandy asked.

"Hell no," Harry said. "Any sensible cocksucker is already fast asleep."

"Just us insensible ones still awake, then."

Harry might have objected to that had he been sober. The Dandy walked over to, and then behind, the bar, looking for bottles. Now that he was closer to the lantern, Harry could see him better. He was young and handsome, with long dark wavy hair. He wore a dark purple brocaded silk waistcoat and fine wool britches, with a white shirt that seemed to have not a speck of dirt on it.

"I beg your pardon," he said, "but do you know where he keeps the brandy?"

"Fuckin' France, most likely," Harry answered, snorting.

"I see."

"To the best of my recollection, Ronnie ain't had a bottled liquor here in over a month. Trade whiskey is the choice you've got, and I am gonna climb way out on a fucking limb and suggest you abstain."

"Hmm," the dandy said, considering. "You'll find I don't much like to abstain from things. Sheriff..."

"Marshall," Harry stopped him. "I'm the Town Marshall. It's a step below Sheriff. The Sheriff don't hardly bother with Clanton."

"Ah. Well then. Marshall..." the dandy stopped. "I'm sorry. I don't happen to know your name."

"Harry Parker."

"Dorian Gray," the dandy replied in turn. "Now what exactly is trade whiskey, if I may ask?"

"That depends," Harry said, "on the honesty and decency of the man who makes it. It's mostly grain liquor, with some burnt sugar and a little tobacco to give it a bead. Ronnie is a sane and mostly sober son of a bitch, so his liquor is not apt to kill you straight off. Some of the kegs he buys off traders on the other hand I cannot vouch for."

"And what are you drinking?" Gray asked him.

"It's called Panther Piss. It's one of the kegs I won't vouch for. I used to be a fucking Quaker until I started in on it, so you may take your decision advisedly."

Harry took a sip off his drink. It never stopped tasting terrible.

Gray took a glass, and examined it casually before pouring himself one. He watched the brown liquor pour out, complete with small flecks of god only knew what. Tobacco, he hoped.

"Notch the keg with that chalk there, would ya, so Ronnie knows what I drank."

Gray nodded and did so, and his eyes went a little wide at the multitude of notches already there.

"You, Mister Parker, are a man of prodigious appetites."

"Well now," Harry said, "that's the nicest way a man has called me a drunk in a long time. Set a spell."

Harry kicked a chair back opposite him so that Gray could sit down. Gray did so, and then took a cautious sip of the liquor. It was clear that it was not what he had been expecting. In Harry's experience it had never once been what he'd expected either. Every glass seemed to bring new miseries. To his credit, Gray's eyes did not immediately fill with tears as he had seen happen to tougher looking men.

"That is truly, truly, the worst thing I've ever put in my body," Gray said, "If you knew how widely I've traveled, and how open to new experiences I am, you'd have more respect for the statement."

"Hell," Harry said, "I only drink it because I think it'll prepare me for hell."

Gray hesitated before he took another sip.

"Does it improve with repeated sips?" he asked.

"Nope, but after five or six, your tongue dies of pure horror, and you can't taste it anymore."

Gray smiled, and took the sip.

"May I ask what you were working at when I came in. I don't mean to intrude."

Harry felt a small twitch at the corner of his eye. He was used to having to fight a man when he talked about poetry. He pushed the urge down. This man seemed all right.

"I was working," Harry said, with as much dignity as his drunkenness would allow, "on my poetry."

That was clearly not the answer Gray had been expecting. Something in his eyes changed. There was no mockery in those eyes at all. He had come over more human all of a sudden, and less of a performer.

"I have known many poets," Gray said, "Some intimately. Do you know the work of the Irish playwright Oscar Wilde?"

"I've heard of him, sure."

"He's an acquaintance of mine. It was on his recommendation that I chose to visit America. He found his trip here most exciting."

"Nice place to visit, but you wouldn't want to live there."

"I meant no offense."

"None taken. I reckon I'd feel the same way about England. I once thought I wanted to live there, but now I'm sure it's just another place. Ain't likely any better or worse than here. Just fancier."

"You're quite right there, Mr. Parker. In London, my worst enemies smile and shake my hand, but behind my back they work at my destruction. Things seem more honest here, at least."

"Mostly. Snakes everywhere, just the same. No matter where you go."

The two men had a moment of easy quiet as they each took another small sip of Panther Piss. They both grimaced and smiled at one another in kind.

"Mr. Parker, I don't mean to be impertinent, but would you be so kind as to read me one of your poems. You are the most unusual man I've ever seen to call himself such, and I find it fascinating."

Harry shifted in his seat uncomfortably, and rubbed the back of his neck with a palm.

"Hell, I don't know. I don't think they'd be up to the standard you're used to with Mr. Wilde."

"Few men are up to that standard. There's no shame in that, I'm quite sure. Please. I do insist."

Harry closed his eyes tight.

"Fine, but if you laugh, I'll shoot you square in the forehead."

Gray smiled.

"On my honour as a gentleman."

"All right then. This ain't finished, mind you. I been working on it some time now. Nights mostly. While piss-drunk."

"Of course."
Harry cleared his throat and read.

CHAPTER SEVEN

The Ballad of Harry Parker, by Arise-Ye-Sons-of-Israel Parker

TO START, I GOT A better deal than most
    In this life you die alone, you're born alone;
    the first and last, the hardest posts
    I was born with a brother to push me out the hole
    His name was John, and he tricked me good
    I birthed first, he died first, may God rest his soul
    He was seven years old when the cart reared back
    I was just inside the store, paying for feed
    He died in the street from a broken back
    The first long year, it was the worst
    Long black nights alone, my mother cried
    My father too, but the farm came first
    We toiled through pain, our faces grim
    The tyranny of the crops was absolute
    There was no other choice for him
    Once the work was through we headed west
    Sill Creek, Ohio Christians all
    Leaving ghosts behind, and hoping for the best
    I was a dreamer then, a child
    Fancied I would be a poet
    Leave this country, young and wild
    I dreamed of sailing, seeing Wales
    To walk among the streets so old
    As were recounted in my father's tales
    My only friend was a boy named Gus

Giant-tall, but hunched, half-lame
No two friends had ever laughed as much as us
His twisted back set him apart
Me, my funny name, my Quaker faith
He chose to call me Harry, bless his heart
He had dreams of heading west, a six-gun at his side
A rusted piece of shit he found in the ditch
He cleaned it up, and showed it off with pride
He set it in my hands one day as we
Hid out in the woods near his father's cows
It was so much heavier than I thought it'd be
It was a simple tool to kill a man
Iron, lead, gunpowder nothing more
It was natural, balanced, felt good in my hand
Quakers, they believe in peace
And I was then a Quaker still
It shook me so, that I could kill with ease
He asked me to come along
on his journey to the wooly west
I told him he was simple, and that his dreams were wrong
It was the worst thing I have done in life
And I've killed half a dozen men at least
Caused untold misery and strife
The men in his family did not live long
Their chests were twisted in and bent
He wanted a life spoke of in song
Instead his Daddy died when he was seventeen
And he took up the farm to feed his kin
Settled in for a life mundane and mean
I helped him for awhile, as best I could
Spent that long winter in their house
You can't fix a life by fetching wood
He'd had a choice of deaths, under yoke, or by the gun
I'd latched him to the pulling beasts
Like some dark god, I'd snuffed his sun
The light and life they left him then
He only lived to sow and till
And knew he'd die, but just cared when
He had to last as long as it took

His brother to grow and take his place
I wished he'd left and been a crook
Farms eat men, as men eat wheat
They grind them down
And leave us rotten meat
In the dead of night, a coward it would seem
I stole a horse, dug up his gun
And rode away to steal his dream
Since that time I've made my fame
by killing men and stealing gold
Never once have I used my name
Arise, he died there in the woods
I left him under the stone for Gus
And Harry Parker left the Quaker life for good
Father, he would die of shame if he knew the things I've done
My mother probably thinks I'm dead
But Gus must know I stole his gun

CHAPTER EIGHT

Clanton, Colorado 1880

"THERE'S A LITTLE MORE, BUT it ain't worth spending breath on," Harry said.

Gray leaned back in his chair, his eyes moist.

"You surprise me, sir."

Harry narrowed his eyes trying to decipher the meaning in Gray's words. He felt the near involuntary movement of his hand toward his gun. He knew if he shot an unarmed Englishman, he'd dance at the end of a rope. It was a dance he was willing to do rather than face mockery.

"What do you mean, I surprise you?" Harry asked, more than a hint of danger in his words.

"I surely mean no offense," Gray said, "I am not, myself, a poet, but I would not have expected... I confess, I'm at something of a loss to express what I mean to say."

"Did you like the fucking thing, or did you not?"

"Emphatically, I did," Gray said. "The language may be a bit rough-hewn, and I'm not entirely sure of the scansion in one or two of the stanzas, but the emotion is most clearly communicated."

"All right then," Parker said, relaxing somewhat. He'd just, for some reason spilled his fucking heart to this stranger, and he was raw about it.

"I'm a mite rusty, I admit."

Gray waved his hand dismissively.

"The flaws are part of what lets it breathe," he said. "Change not a word."

"I reckon I'll have to," Harry said, "As I understand it, a poem needs every word and beat just so."

"Precision," Gray said, "is fine for clocks, but it's not, in my experience, part of the human condition."

Harry thought on that for a few minutes, and realized there was a lot of truth in it. Part of why his poems had never seemed to match his expectations is that they weren't half as messy nor as bloody as a broken heart.

"You're not as much of a joke as you look, Gray," Harry said, straight-faced.

"No," he said, "I'm much worse."

Harry laughed. It was a fine quality, when a man could laugh at himself. It was a quality he'd had once, and it had gone missing. It was probably with his eternal soul. At least it'd keep warm.

"Mr. Parker..."

"Hell, call me Harry."

"I won't, I think," Gray said, with a slightly sad look to his eyes.

Harry shrugged, and went to the barrel for more whiskey.

"Arise," Gray said, "is a lovely name."

Harry tensed.

"Don't fucking use that name, Gray."

"Call me Dorian, won't you?"

Harry turned to look at him, glass full again.

"Gray's much the prettier name, cocksucker."

Harry batted his eyes at the Englishman comically.

"Mr. Parker, then," Gray said.

Harry nodded and came back to the table, turning the chair around to mount it backwards. He set the glass on the table, and put his arms across the back of the chair, resting his chin on them.

"Mr. Parker," Gray continued, "I can't help but think that you've shared something rather painful and private with me. I haven't the first idea why."

"That makes fuckin' two of us then," Harry said, not looking at him, but instead at the saloon door. "Probably, I'm just drunk."

"Well, you have my word that I'll not tell a soul."

"Who the fuck you gonna tell?" Harry said, "The queen of England. She don't give a shit about either of my names."

"I want to share a secret with you, sir. I have a secret of my own. If you're a coward, then so am I. You've run from your farm, and I've run away from death itself."

"No shame in running from death," Harry said.

"You don't understand. I will never die. I cannot die."

"Bet you will," Harry said, with a smirk. "but I remember when I was your age. I don't think I believed it either."

"How old do you think that I am?"

"I reckon you might be twenty-five, or thereabouts."

"I'm sixty-one this April, sir."

Harry laughed.

"Oh hell," he said, "I might have known you were drunk, considering. You're surely a sober-seeming kind of a drunk."

"I am stone sober," Gray said. "I have made a bargain with death. I cannot die. Nearly thirty years ago, I met a man who offered me unending youth. He made a kind of paint from my blood, and from his own. With it, he painted a picture of me as I was then. That painting resides in a closet in my home, now. I stay entirely young and free of flaw, but the painting grows older. With each wicked deed I perform it grows more terrible to look upon. I, on the other hand, am only corrupted within. This satisfies my vanity, but leaves me with an emptiness I cannot seem to fill with drink or sex, nor any kind of pleasure."

"Crazy story," Harry said, "I reckon you believe it."

"Every word," Gray said, "I assure you."

"Well, if you ever get tired of it, you can always blow your brains out. I've seen plenty of fucking men do it."

"I've considered it," Gray said, "but I lack the courage, and I don't know that it would work."

"Trust me," Harry said dryly. "It does."

"You misunderstand. Let me show you."

Gray picked up his shot glass and slammed it into the table, where it went to shards. The noise caused Harry to startle, and his hand again to move for his gun before relaxing. Gray removed his jacket and proceeded to roll up his sleeve. With an almost theatrical flourish, he picked up a shard of broken glass, and he slowly cut a wound open in his arm from wrist to elbow. The blood flowed onto the dirty sawdust strewn floor, and tears ran from the corners of Gray's eyes.

Harry stood up to hold the dumb fuck down and render succour, as he was clearly out of his cotton-picking mind, and not able to govern himself sensibly. Before Harry could move, the blood seemed to crawl back under the skin. It was replaced by a flow of quicksilver that receded back through the skin and left no mark whatsoever behind.

There was not even blood left except what had hit the floor. He stared at the blood on the floor.

"I've suffered worse injuries by far," Gray said. "With no more lasting effect."

The blood on the floor shimmered, and rolled together, changing colour as it did to a mirror finish. Then, as he held down the urge to scream, the blood started to move. Like tiny beetles, the drops of blood crawled together and formed into one puddle of flowing mirror. Harry felt rooted to the place where he stood. Gray knelt down, and offered his hand to the shining puddle. It crawled up onto his hand like a tamed squirrel, and stayed there.

"What the fuck?" Harry said, "What kind of fucking witchcraft is this?"

"I don't know," Gray answered. "I've never known."

"What the fuck is that stuff? It sure as hell ain't any natural quicksilver."

Gray stared at the silver in his hand.

"No," Gray said. "It isn't. You know, I've looked into a pool of it before. It's not just reflective. I can see all manner of things in it..."

Gray stopped short and turned his head away. The stuff, whatever it was melted back into him like it had never been there.

"I cannot recommend you look at it."

"No fucking worries there," Harry said. "As soon as you are the fuck out of my town, I don't expect I'll ever have to. Can't possibly be soon enough at this point."

Harry was possessed of something like a genuine fear of the devil for the first time since he was a boy. He wanted to shoot Gray, put an end to him, this thing that should not be. He only stayed his hand out of the near certainty it would not work.

Before he could even reconsider, Gray was standing in front of him, close enough that he could see each one of his fine eyelashes, close enough that he could see Gray had no pores on his skin at all. He looked more like a doll than a man at this remove. Gray took a hold of his wrists and held them with a strength that shocked and scared him. Gray pushed him down to his knees and Harry made a sound of protest, but could not resist. Gray was inhumanly strong.

"You've a poet's heart, and beautiful eyes, Arise-Ye-Sons-Of-Israel," Gray said. "The world is prettier with you in it."

Gray retched, his stomach heaving, and something drew up from the bowels of him, and then the silver flowed from his opened mouth, and his nose, flowing like honey down over Harry's face. It was cold as it touched him, and heavy. He could feel it squirm up his nostrils, between his pursed tight lips, and even in through the corners of his eyes. It made him feel weak and timeless, and the invasion seemed to last forever.

Gray released him and Harry fell to the floor, clawing and ripping at his own flesh as the cold heavy gutsilver moved through him, dragging him into a deep and dreamless sleep.

By the time Harry woke from his gasping dream, Gray was gone, and so was his own death.

CHAPTER NINE

Clanton, Colorado 1881

FUCKING POLACK IDIOTS SHOULD HAVE known better than to draw on him, Harry reckoned. If they'd thrown down their irons when he'd told them to, they would, both of them, still be alive. Instead, they were stacked up like firewood on the floor of the jailhouse. The room stank of blood and shit and death. Harry was sitting at the desk, drinking from the broken neck of a bottle of whiskey he'd found in Wojeck's saddlebags. The bottle had taken a bullet, the horse too, poor fucking thing. There was blood down the side of the smoked glass. Still, he wasn't going to let real whisky go undrunk on a night when he'd killed a horse. And some men.

His shirt and pants were full of holes and stained with blood. Most of that was his from when the bullets struck. He'd taken four or five during the exchange of fire. That was plain embarrassing to the shooters. They must have shot off close to a hundred rounds at him. He'd fired three. He was a fair shot, but it was hard to miss when you could just walk right up to a man and shoot him in the chest.

The thing he'd learned about bullets was that they hurt like a son of a bitch, but they didn't really have the push to knock a man down. Pain is what knocked a man down, mostly, or simple damage. Shotguns, provided they had a heavy enough load, were enough to slow a man down some, but only some. If the pain and the damage were no longer a real obstacle, then you could pretty much ignore bullets. As long as he hovered somewhere between drunk and blind drunk, he could advance on the fucking cavalry until they pulled out their cannons.

He took another hit from the bottle, the jagged edge coming away with crimson and silver lines on the cutting edges. He couldn't feel it. He only had the barest idea where his own feet were.

The Wojeck brothers had been trouble for Harry Parker. They had been in Clanton for as long as there'd been a Clanton. Stan and Paul farmed just outside of town, potatoes and Indian corn, mostly. They kept cattle. Ed was in and out of town, working the nearby mines most of the time, coming home at harvest, and on occasional pleasure trips. He'd known them all since he'd first come to town. They were decent folk who got on well with people despite the fact they were heathen idol-worshipping Catholics. He'd seen towns where that alone would have made them fucking outcasts, but Clanton was not that kind of a town. Hell, even the Mormons got on all right here.

Harry would never have guessed he'd wind up having to shoot any of them, let alone all three. Mind you, he'd never have guessed that a pansy from England would blow through town and turn him into a fucking monster neither. Life was full of all manner of interesting surprises.

Even now, he thought he could hear the townsfolk in their little houses, and whispering in the saloon, talking about how the Wojeck brothers had been right, and that he was sent by the devil to devour them. He was afraid he would have to shoot some more folks before the night was over.

The trouble had started half a year ago when Ed Wojeck had seen Harry take a bullet to the back. It was an ordinary saloon scuffle that got out of hand, and a drunk miner named Morrison had let a shot go. Harry sold it as just a graze, and delivered a sound beating to Morrison, who sure as hell never meant to actually fire, and left it at that.

Harry never imagined things could go so poorly from there, but Wojeck had started in almost immediately with crazy talk of how Harry was a vampire sent by the devil. Soon, there was all kinds of whisper that it was true, and all kinds of whispers it was bullshit.

It would have stopped there except Stan's daughter Sofie started ailing from a kind of anemia. She fell pale and weak, and eventually, that morning, had died.

Harry knew full well that he had feasted on nobody's blood, but he had a harder time denying that he was of the devil, or claiming he was just a normal man. And to have the girl die of a blood disease was a stroke of plain terrible luck, and not for just the girl.

The Wojecks had shown up at the jailhouse just around dark, demanding he surrender himself. They were half-mad with their own grief, and not thinking clearly. No man is going to surrender to being killed, which is surely what they had in mind. He'd heard them talk before of what you did to a vampire. He wasn't one, but he was powerfully sure that having your head cut off and the rest of you burned was pretty much fatal to whatever walked on two feet. If it wasn't fatal to him, he was pretty sure he'd have been gladder if it were.

He'd leaned out the window and told them to throw their guns down. They'd told him to come out and go to hell. So he had opened the door, and they fired and fired again at him, missing to the point of absurdity, likely all three drunk as hell.

Harry had walked to them, and fired once at each of them. He missed Ed when a bullet caught his shoulder, and accidentally shot his horse instead. He had cursed, and Ed had departed the scene of the battle on foot, running into the night. Gunfight then over, he dispatched the poor wounded beast.

The townsfolk had seen him take the one in the shoulder, they had to have, so he play-acted his injury, and dragged the dead men into the jail house swearing and grunting, even though they seemed to weigh no more than a baby to him now.

Then he came out for the whiskey he'd seen in the saddlebags. Since then he had been drinking, and trying to decide how best to govern his life. The more he drank, the more he imagined he could hear in the saloon, and in the houses, a constant stream of talk, mostly about him, all of it scared.

He spat, stood up and went out into the street, and he fired his gun twice in the air.

"Listen up, you high-strung cocksuckers! I'm Harry Fucking Parker, and I am the law in this town. I'm sorry as hell I had to shoot these Polacks, but they had lost their damned minds. I will shoot anyone of you cocksuckers who tries the same, be it to me, or to any other decent law-abiding fucking citizen. I am ten feet tall, and I am fucking bulletproof. Any man who has a problem with doing what I fucking say had best step to the street right sharply, or keep his mouth shut!"

His last few words echoed off the tall hills to the north of town.

"No takers?" he shouted. "I fuckin' thought not!"

The town was as quiet as the grave as he walked back into his jailhouse. The door shut behind him, he wiped a hand across his face.

Shaking with adrenaline, drunk, angry and despairing, he knelt down beside and lapped at Stan's wound, just to be sure they weren't right. The taste was bitter and salty. He spat it out.

"You fucking happy, now, you dumb fucks? I told you I wasn't no fucking vampire."

He sat back down in his chair and covered his face with his hands, soul sick and tired. He didn't sleep. He didn't dare tonight.

CHAPTER TEN

Clanton, Colorado 1882

THE YEAR HAD GONE BY with a fearful quiet. He drank alone. People tipped their hats to him in the street, a thing that always rankled, but he let it go. It showed respect. Clanton, to a man, feared him. Most hated him. None could deny, however, that there was rule of law. If you were crazy enough to step outside the lines, Harry Parker either put you back inside those lines, or he took you clean out of the Earth.

The county sheriff had stopped coming to Clanton altogether. For one thing, there was no crime to speak of. Also, Harry had told the officious little cocksucker that the next time he showed up, he'd best bring a troop of Federal Marshalls and a Gatling gun if he wanted to see another sunrise.

Harry was pure trouble and as heavy as lead, but he kept his town clean, and never shot a man who he didn't have claim to it. He wasn't worth the trouble to swat down, with his little fiefdom, and even if he were, the Sheriff was too much in fear to try. This was just as Harry liked it. He'd found that he'd had to shoot at a man once every three months or so. His reputation was such that he drew a certain kind of trouble to town in the form of professional shooters wanting to make their own bones. He just tried not to kill them if he could.

Out-drawing a man was barely a concern for him, but it was inconvenient when people saw him take a round, so he'd studied it. With the gutsilver working at the insides of him, he was fast as a scalded cat. His lack of fear took away the other problem in shooting a man down. What you needed to win a gunfight was the ability to move as fast as you could without fear and nerves messing with your aim.

He was reading the newspaper that had started up a few months back, half for pleasure, and half to make sure the rag hadn't said something he might have to take issue with. He needn't have worried. The thing barely said anything at all to anyone. Empty words muttered to sound important.

There was a knock on the door, and he looked up.

"Come in," he said, hand on his gun, which he kept drawn but held under the desk.

The door creaked open and Eloise McCabe walked in. She was the oldest daughter of the owner of the mercantile, seventeen years old, pale blue eyes and hair the colour of corn-silk. Her cheeks looked fresh washed, but there was a smear on one that looked like soot. It made him want to sit her down and wash her face like she was a toddler. She wore a simple blue dress, and he could just see the little black leather shoes she wore. She kept her eyes down, as scared of him as most people.

"Morning, Marshal Parker," she said.

"Morning, Miss McCabe," he said, tucking the gun in a holster he had nailed to the bottom of his desk. "How can I help you?"

"I don't want to interrupt," she said, "as it's not urgent."

Harry set the paper down, and slid it off to one side of the desk.

"I am doing absolutely nothing of any fucking importance. Beg your pardon."

Eloise blushed as he swore, and Harry found that a little charming. He did curse more than the average man in town, but considering the town was nearly an eighth Mormon, that brought the average down somewhat. Surely, she heard worse every day. Her own father had a salty tongue, he knew for certain.

"This is something of a personal call, Mr. Parker."

Harry raised his eyebrows and fixed his gaze on her. Once in a while, since he'd first come to town, some young filly would take a liking to him. He'd been tempted once or twice, but had resigned himself to the life of a bachelor, and he wasn't about to tarnish any decent girls silly enough to fall for him. Since the change he'd been doubly sure that no mortal woman needed any part of him. For all he knew, his own seed would trap them in the same place he was. He was set apart and half crazy like a wild bear with an itch he couldn't scratch forever. He wouldn't wish it on anyone, let alone a girl of real character like Eloise McCabe. In a town full of mostly decent people, she'd often struck him as one of the kindest. She was the sort of girl who tries to tend to fallen sparrows. She had a world full of pain to discover, poor thing.

"Does your mother know you're here, Eloise?"

She shook her head slightly, and quietly answered, "No."

"Well, then, you'd best say your piece and head on home sharpish. I don't want either one of us to have a general downturn in our reputation."

She smiled and tucked a lock of hair back behind her ear.

"Don't worry, Marshall. I'm not here to declare my undying love for the dark and mysterious lawman."

Harry smiled, and felt himself relax a little.

"Sit down then, if you like."

She did so, carefully tucking her dress under her as she sat. Women had to go through life, it seemed to him, with everything being half again as complicated as it was for men. It didn't seem hardly fair.

She looked up at him and smiled.

"It seems to me, Mr. Parker," she said, "that you are perfectly capable of being polite, and, I'd say, even charming when you mean to be."

"I reckon I can, same as any man."

She shook her head, "No. You know as well as I do that there are a lot of men who can't. I'd say as many as half of them at a guess. Either they never learned any manners, or they found that swinging a fist got them what they wanted faster."

"Miss McCabe, I don't reckon you came over to jaw over human behaviour and natural philosophy with me. I know my reputation."

"So do I. I also know what you order in through my father. Books aren't cheap to ship, but you pay for them. I don't know of many stone killers who love Whitman as much as you do."

"I don't reckon you know as many stone killers as you think you do."

"I don't think I know even one, Mr. Parker. I think you work as hard as you can to make us all think you are pure terror in a human disguise. I think you drink too heavily for a man with no conscience, and I think you're the loneliest man I've ever seen."

Harry had nothing to say for a second.

"Just what in the actual hell do you want, Elly?"

"I just want to know what makes a man pull away so hard from the world that he nearly breaks his own neck. And, if you'll take it, I want to offer you the hand of friendship. Strange as you are, the people here are good people, and they're ready to like you again if you'd just let them try."

Harry looked at her earnest face, not sure exactly when seventeen years old had come to be the same as six years old to him, and he smiled.

"Get the fuck out of my jailhouse," he said. "When I want friends, I'll go looking for them someplace without the local measure of cousin marriage."

She did not flinch, and considering the fear and awe he had come to inspire, his heart ached at the purity of her spirit. He could only just barely remember that kind of passion and bravery and faith in the human spirit.

"That isn't going to work on me," she said. "I'm on to you."

He stood up.

"Don't make me call your parents. Scat."

She stood up with dignity, and did not look away.

"I'm here if you change your mind, Mr. Parker. We all are."

She crossed to the door.

"Don't hold your fucking breath, missy."

"Don't die from your own spite," she said back, leaving on the last word, which was, as he dimly recalled, the custom of women.

He opened the drawer and took a slow sip of whiskey.

CHAPTER ELEVEN

Clanton, Colorado 1882

HARRY WAS FACE DOWN ON his desk, hands slack at his sides. He'd drunk himself straight into oblivion and was dead to the world in dreamless sleep. He was jerked back awake when a foot nudged his chair. Sitting bolt upright, he grabbed the gun from under his desk, looked up and pointed it right at the man nearest.

There were four of them, standing in the jailhouse. The one nearest was close to seven feet tall, and broad as a bull. Unlike his childhood friend, there was no stooping, no hunch, only a sense of total invincibility. He was naked to the waist, except for a comically small bowler hat that sat on top of his bald head. He wore denim pants and black boots, and a gun on each hip. He had small black moustaches and eyes the colour of fresh grown roses. He smiled with teeth showing, and despite the gun pointed at his face, he had no fear. He looked, in fact, like a man that had never known any fear at all in his life. By the door was a preacher, thin and reedy, about Harry's height. His white collar had little flecks of dried blood on it. His hair was brown, and messy enough that Harry doubted it had seen a brush in years. Leaning on the bars of the cell was a smiling city slicker dressed in an eastern suit. He wore no hat. His black hair was slicked down and parted in the middle. He had pencil thin moustaches that made him look French. Lastly, sitting on the chair where Eloise had most recently sat, was a woman in a red dress. It showed off, to considerable success, both cleavage and ankle. Her jet black hair was pulled back and to the side, and in her hair was a lily flower, a strange choice, funereal and dark. She wore too much makeup, and her skin was Mexican dark, but painted pale with powder. Whether he ought to keep his eye on the giant son of a bitch in the bowler, or give in to his baser lusts, and stare at the lady in red was a hard choice.

"Back up several fucking steps," Harry said to the giant, "unless you want a new hole to piss out of."

The giant smiled and made a fist, every knuckle cracking as he did so. He had the look of a man itching to smash in a face, but he inclined his head to the lady. She nodded to him. The giant shrugged and stepped back, his hands raised halfway up, more to mock than show obeisance.

"Too bad," the giant said, "It's fun to crack the skull of a man who can't die. You get to do it so many times."

"Who the fuck are you people?" Harry said.

"My name is Holden, but people call me The Judge." the giant said. "The preacher there is named John. The other gentleman is Jules. The lady here, who is our wife, is Esperanza."

"I think, lady," I said to her in her own language, "that you could hope for better than this tub of guts."

"You speak Spanish," she said, her voice free of any accent he knew.

"A little."

She smiled.

"Now what the hell do you want from me?"

"Like you, none of us can die," the judge spoke. "Word of your successes here have reached the ears of..my boss. He sent us to talk to you."

"I see," Harry said, smiling, "Are you the law then, come around at last for Mr. Parker's son?"

Esperanza was the first to laugh, and it was near musical, if music was ever so cold. The Judge laughed next, his considerable belly shaking up and down. The preacher kept his quiet, and his eyes on just beyond the door. Jules looked at him, and at the others with the cold and unfeeling eye of a seagull.

"Hell no," the Judge said. "We ain't the law. We are in no fucking way the law."

"Then what?"

"We're a recruiting party for a volunteer army, preparing to go into battle with the devil himself," Esperanza said, with the fervent edge of the true believer.

"Are you people missionaries?" he asked with incredulity.

They all said no quite firmly except the preacher, who said, "Yes."

They all turned their heads to look at him with their mouths open in something like surprise. Holden shook his head.

"You know, preacher, you speak so rarely, and yet it always shocks me whenever you do," Holden said.

"Well," said the preacher, "we are. We're missionaries and we're soldiers. When your enemy is the devil, and you seek to recruit soldiers, you're both. There no sense in dissembling."

"He's right," Esperanza said, "he's right. We're both."

"Well," Harry said, "I ain't much interested in going to war or signing up for a religion or a fuckin' army. I've got my responsibilities here, and that's plenty for me."

"Hell," the Judge spoke, "We have no interest in spoiling your little kingdom here, or in the people live here. We just want you to ride with us a spell, let us show you some things and get you educated before you make your decisions."

"Surely, my dear," Esperanza said, "you must have many questions about what's happened to you, and what you've become. We can give you some of those answers. Not every answer you need, I'm sure, but a start."

Harry had considered before if this time might come. If there was Gray and there was him, there must be more. He'd never seen any colour or creed of human being that did not seem to form committees and governments if they could. And here, it seemed, were representatives from whatever passed for a government for creatures like him.

"And if I decide that what you're selling is not for me?" he asked.

"Then you can fuck right back off to this shit-hole town," Holden spoke. "What do we care?"

"All we can do," the preacher said, "is try to show you the truth as we see it. Your choice, then, is your own."

Harry looked Jules in the eye.

"You got anything to say, Frenchie?"

The Frenchman smiled and shook his head side to side.

"Jules don't talk much," the Judge said, "but he is the best man in the world to have at your back in a fight."

Harry felt some degree of challenge in that, and then some shame at being a petty man. Bad enough to be a killer and a drunk, without he take pride in it.

"How the hell long will this take?" he asked Esperanza.

"At most, six weeks. If we are lucky, and the weather is with us. Do you have a horse?"

"I do. He's the gray stallion out back."

"He's very beautiful," Esperanza said.

"He's my horse," Harry said, "not my wife."

Holden laughed. Esperanza smiled.

"Will you do it? Will you come with us?" she asked him.

"Give me a minute to think. Alone, will you?"

She nodded, and rose. As one unit they seemed to move to the door, closing it behind them. Harry leaned back in his chair, and struggled with himself. He was used to making sudden decisions and dealing with the consequences. Usually these consequences were only his own. For over a year, though, he'd been the sole source of law and order. No deputies served under him, as they weren't needed, and he didn't want to deal with them. If he left for six weeks, he'd be leaving the town lawless. He was not sure how long his reputation would be enough to maintain the peace.

On the other hand, he reckoned that this might be his only chance to find out what that fucking pansy had done to him, and what gutsilver was, maybe even what it meant. They might have all manner of answers to all manner of questions. He was fair to certain they wouldn't offer twice. And more, he did not feel right about these people. He was most especially concerned about the Judge, and by Jules, who had the look to him especially of a man who liked to hurt people. He half suspected that saying no would have consequences to his town that he would not find pretty. Time riding with them deferred those consequences a spell until such time as he had some understanding, however vague, of his predicament. It would also take them away from his town. He was a monster, so that the folk who lived there didn't have to deal with many and he didn't have to deal with them.

Letting out a deep breath, he walked out the front of the jailhouse.

"I'll go," he said to the four of them, who were leaning against the rail of the boardwalk next to the hitching post where all four of their horses were arrayed. They looked, riders and horses alike, like the dream of people more than people themselves, like something out of a storybook.

"I'm glad," Esperanza said.

He nodded.

"I'll need a minute."

"Take your time," Holden says. "The horses need a rest anyhow."

Harry walked across the street to the saloon. The drinkers looked up at him, and Ronnie too, expecting trouble, for that's when he tended to arrive.

"Listen up," Harry spoke to the assembled. "I been called away as part of a posse. I can't, in any way, say no. I could be gone for six weeks. I'm therefore forced to rely upon you drunken cocksuckers to keep to law and order here. So spread the word. Should any of you stray from the path of righteousness, I will, on my return, fill you so full of lead that your fat heads won't float. See if I don't."

Harry turned to leave, and nobody said a word.

Within the hour, he and the others were on the trail to wherever it was they were taking him. Utah, they said.

CHAPTER TWELVE

Colorado 1882

BEAR-ON-FIRE SAT ON a mountain, his legs crossed, and his eyes closed. There was no grass this high up, and so he sat on stone. It was cold, but he no longer felt the cold. The air was thin, but he was strong enough to breathe. It was quiet up here, aside from the wind. It was too high even for the birds. For a few moments, he had peace inside his own head.

He did not know why he had come to Colorado, except that he felt a pull to go there, as though the sky metal inside of him was pulled to more of its kind. He sensed there was a gathering, of sorts. He had never felt such a pull before, nor sensed so much sky metal gathering in a place. He did not know if he wished to join such a gathering, but he felt the strong need to be near it.

He had seen, in the last ten years, more of the gods, those with the sky metal in them. He had learned that all were not the same. They had in common that they would not die, could not die, in fact. Some were strong, and others fast. Some could leap, and others swim like the seals. Some could read minds or change their face.

Only he could do all of these things, and he did not know why. Only he, as far as he knew, had fallen from the sky. He knew that he might find answers if he only spoke to them, that not all of them would necessarily flee from contact. He'd seen some hand in hand. Yet he did not approach them.

There was no good reason for it. It was simple human frailty. He was shy. He'd spent too long away from his People, and from people in general. He'd forgotten, nearly, how to talk, and sometimes it felt as though his thoughts were now too big to condense down into words. On the few occasions he had been spoken to by the people he'd helped, they spoke to him with fear and reverence, the same tone that the white man used when he prayed to his God. Even if he had wanted to rejoin the company of men, he doubted he could. He had grown too large in deeds, and too small in heart and feeling.

There was a part of him that wondered if he might be able to sit on this mountain top forever, as peaceful and constant as any stone. Without the sounds and the thoughts of men pressing in on him, would he be able to just lie back and sleep until moss and grass grew over him?

He half suspected that he could. He knew he wouldn't. He was sent from the sky by someone, for some purpose, and he would fulfill that destiny. He had as little choice in the matter as any man. Whatever action he took, his destiny would find him, even here on this mountain.

CHAPTER THIRTEEN

The Green River Trail 1882

THEY HAD SET UP CAMP for the night, in sight of the river. The night was clear, and the stars and moon threw almost enough light to read by, if he'd been so inclined. The talk so far had extended mostly to where they were going which was a farm in Utah territory, inside what the locals called Deseret to the mixed feelings of the federal government. Aside from that, Esperanza and the Judge had talked mostly of some book they'd recently read. He himself had not read this book, and so the conversation had no more meaning to him than if they'd spoken another language. Frenchie didn't speak. The preacher sang hymns as the rode. For the sake of old times, Harry joined in on the ones he knew. It passed the time.

Since setting up camp, they got the workings of a fire together, and their horses were at the water drinking, then grazing closer up. Holden seemed to be a passable camp cook and had potatoes boiling in a pot atop the fire, as the sun fell behind the mountains and the summer night got that little bit less comfortable.

Esperanza had ridden side-saddle most of the way, but she had clearly had her fill of that. She stepped into the bushes and came back wearing a sensible pair of trousers, with a belt she'd had to add notches in. The pants were too big for her, and should have made her look the fool, but to him it added appeal. She seemed prettier now that she wasn't trying so hard. After a few hours of riding, everyone had their edges worn down a little. Even the Frenchman had a slack, tired look to his face that made him look less hungry.

"So," Harry said, "You promised me some wisdom you had on offer."

57

"We did," the Judge said, leaning back on one hand, and scratching his belly with the other. "Just hard for a man to know where to start."

"There's a lot to tell," Esperanza said, "What do you most want to know?"

"Am I bound for hell? Is this the devil's seed in me?"

The Preacher leaned forward, wrapping his arms around his knees.

"No," he said. "What's in you is no more the devil than this campfire is hell. It is what it is. What you do with it determines your fate."

"How the hell do you know that?"

"God has spoken to me. I'm His prophet."

"I see," Harry said, "so what you're telling me is that you don't fucking know it. It's your goddamned religion tells you so?"

"I know it," the preacher said, "and I'm not alone. He has spoken to others."

Harry sighed. He'd been worried about this, that the wisdom he'd get was a fairy story they'd all agreed on just the way normal folk agreed to believe in Jesus and the cross. It let them sleep nights, and regulated their natural inclination to wicked bastardry.

"Look," he said, turning to the Judge. "He's a preacher, and clearly you folk share his religion, but you don't strike me as particularly god-fearing. Do you know what this shit is inside of me?"

"You're talking about the anima, the ectoplasm, the soul mirror?"

"I'm talking about the fuckin' silver in my blood and bones."

"The very same," the Judge said.

"Yeah then, that's what I'm asking about."

"These are the facts. This is what we know," said the Judge.

CHAPTER FOURTEEN

The Judge

THESE ARE THE FACTS. THIS is what we know.

There's a lot of conjecture, and a lot of theories. There are philosophies and dissertations. There are rumours and allegations. There are even religions and dogmas. No two undying men seem to agree with each other completely on the nature of what's come over us. These are the things we know.

Whatever has happened has happened before in the distant past. We have folktales and legends of immortal men with powers and abilities beyond the realm of the purely natural. Back to the classical times of Egypt and Rome and Greece. The tales of Heracles, and the oracle at Delphi, the Celtic giant Cuchulcain, the Russian witch, the Baba Yaga. So we know that this has happened before.

We know as well that none of us are so old as them. We have searched the corners of the world, and shared what we have found and not one of us predates the fall of the Stone. We know that the ones who came before have gone away. Each of us can trace ourselves back to the fall of that Damned Stone. So we know as well, that the stone is where we start.

In the year of our Lord 1751, there was an incident in which a great stone fell from the sky. Some say it was a comet, loosing part of itself, and that its cyclical travel explains the coming and going of the ones who came before, but we do not know the truth of that. That is speculation, and we are looking for truth. We know only that something fell and that it fell near Gibraltar.

Sailors set out to see where it seemed to have landed, and some three hundred miles to the northwest of Africa they found an island nobody had ever seen. Settlers came at once seeking living space, no more than a hundred men and their families. Five years later, the island bled out its silver blood. All died save twenty. The twenty had somehow been changed by it where the rest had taken ill and passed. These twenty could not die. They made a pact to leave the Island, called the Salt Mouse Island, on account of its shape and the abundance of salt thereon, and tell nobody what had happened. It was too dangerous, and too risky, and any man who could might risk his life for the reward of eternal life.

Nobody knows who first found that they could safely share that reward, and nobody can blame them for trying. Each of these men and women, you must understand, had taken their chances on the Salt Mouse Island, and each of them had lost their friends, and their families. These souls wandered alone in the world. Those who had tried to take their own lives in despair had found no way to do so.

Twenty made twenty more, and twenty more by them. Now there are perhaps ten thousand of us, and maybe there are more. There has been no census taken, and probably there never will be.

It's at this time now, at the edge of the new millennium, that we have, as a group, seemed to turn inward and consider the implications. Societies have formed, and they do not all agree. Some feel we might be best served by limiting our numbers, others say that every man and woman should be saved. Each of us must come to their own decisions.

An ending will come. If those heroes who came before are gone, then where have they gone? If they are dead, does this imply that the effect is temporary, or merely that there are ways to die we do not know?

On this we have no answers. We have only guesses and opinions.

This much we know; In 1751, the Stone fell, and was called the Salt Mouse Island. In 1800 or thereabouts, the stone bled silver and all but twenty died. These twenty have shared the silver with normal men and changed them too.

All the rest is chaos and conjecture, and the fuel for war. When two men argue, it is because one of them, or both of them are ignorant.

This is what we know: Nearly fucking nothing.

CHAPTER FIFTEEN

Green River Trail 1882

"YOU FUCKING REHEARSE THAT?" HARRY asked, looking at the Judge with doubt.

"I'm accustomed," said the Judge, "to sudden bouts of extemporizing and profundity and also sudden savage bursts of pure inhuman violence. I'd like to blame my condition, but that would be a lie. I was always a glorious bastard, and I'm the only one I know of who stole the silver. I took it from a Spaniard during the Mexican War."

"So that's all there is to it. No act of god, no ancient fucking mystery. A fucking rock fell from the sky and when it cracked open some poor sons of bitches got its blood on them. That's our fucking story?"

"No," the preacher said. "As Holden told you, that is just what we know to be true. It's not all the truth there is."

"What is truth?" Harry said, with a satisfied smirk on his face. The preacher grinned.

"Well, someone must be right," the preacher said.

"I doubt it," Harry said.

They were quiet then around the fire for a time. The preacher, whose name, Harry had not once forgotten, was John, seemed to be reconsidering his approach to the discussion. The Judge looked like a man who was a bit bored with the discussion. The Frenchman was falling asleep. Esperanza was the only one of them with a mind still on the conversation.

"Have you ever heard of one of us dying?" Harry asked her.

She shook her head, and frowned.

"No," she said. "I've never seen one die. I've seen them beg for death, burned so bad it took months for them to heal. But I've seen them come back from ash and bone. The silver seems to hide in the bones if it needs to."

Harry nodded, and scratched burning off his mental list of things that might kill him.

"And if the head's cut off?"

"I don't know," she said, and looked at the others.

"Head grows a new body," the Judge said. "Takes a week or so."

Harry had learned a lot in a short time. Practically as much as he felt he needed to know. The Judge had too quick a fucking answer to that, and it didn't seem to fuss him as much as it had fussed Esperanza when she spoke of burning.

"Jesus, that's near as much as I think I can fucking take in for one night," Harry said.

"Thank god for that," said the Judge. "I'm tired and fucking horny."

Esperanza slapped him on the shoulder, but the slap turned into something more like a caress and he winked at her.

Awkwardly, Harry stepped back from the fire a bit, and he got into his roll, and tried to sleep. He'd no reason to fear them tonight. Whatever they wanted from him, they hadn't gotten it yet.

Holden and his wife, if wife she truly was, seemed to share the same roll, from the sound of it. Playful growls and giggles came clear to him in the still night air and turned to sounds of passion. He listened to her soft moans and Spanish whispers, and to the Judge's grunting, his beastly fucking grunting, like a hog in rut. He pushed his head down as best he could to block it out. It seemed shameful for them to fuck like that where all the rest could hear, especially a preacher. It also made him feel as lonely as ever. He hadn't so much as fingered a whore in three years, and was feeling a strong urge for the first time since he was changed. She was pretty, and seemed kind, and deserved better than that lousy sack of guts. Eventually they stopped, and he got some sleep.

The next morning, he woke early and heard the sound of Esperanza in ecstasy again. He hesitated to poke his head out, out of some desire to preserve decency. That urge did not last long, for he had, most urgently, to piss. If they wanted to rut without shame, then he would smother his own, and piss freely.

As he shook off his roll, he was more than slightly surprised to see that Esperanza was on her hands and knees, being entered from the back by the Frenchie. The Frenchie was pounding away with his hips but seemed to take no more pleasure from it than he would a good shit, and maybe less. Harry could not help but stare a moment. The Judge was in the river up to his waist, just the top of his ass still above the water, washing himself. If he heard his wife making a fucking cuckold of him, he showed no signs. The preacher was at his prayers on both knees. He was peering into an inverted hat, set on a stump. He was mumbling into it in some language Harry did not know.

The judge turned around, and you could see his bushy black pubic hair just above the water. He looked at them on the shore, and at his wife, and he laughed, waving good morning to Harry. His laugh was full of joy, and still there was danger in it. He hesitated to wonder what brought these people joy. Harry knew that the Judge had seen it now, but he had not so much as budged.

Harry pissed into the bushes, and by the time he came back, the Frenchie was wiping himself off, and tucking it away. Esperanza was in her riding pants.

"...not fair," she said with a smile, "I have to sit on that all day you know."

She was as shameless about it as any whore he'd ever known. Perhaps that was it. Yet, he did not see the Frenchman pay her, nor pay the Judge when he came back. He'd seen that before, a husband pimping out his own wife. It was a despicable fucking thing, but it would not have surprised him.

The priest poured the contents of the hat out upon the ground, and Harry saw it had been filled with the gutsilver. The preacher knelt down and lapped it up like a cat, saying, "Amen" at every lick. His stomach churned.

He took the Judge aside as the rest packed up their horses. Holden looked bemused as he was taken off by the river.

"Look," Harry said, "I'm not in any fuckin' position to judge no man, but that French fucker was diddling your wife in the light of day, and you don't nohow seem put out. I don't mean to disrespect you, but I can only guess at the why. So I'll ask you straight, is your wife a whore?"

The Judge laughed, "Why, you interested?"

Harry fixed him a cool glare, trying to keep his temper. It was easier after a whole night and most of a day without whiskey.

"I'm just asking because it's fucking peculiar, and I like not to wander in the dark like a blind fucking pigeon."

"She's not a whore, Harry. She's his wife too. And the preacher's wife."

"She's what now?"

"We're Mormons, Harry, Jesus. I'd have thought you figured that out by now. What with him peering in his goddamned hat and all."

Harry knew some Mormons, some through traveling, and some from Clanton. None in his town had been the sort to have more than one wife. They had seemed to think the ones who did were trouble, and that it was no kind of good thing for the wives, nor, in most respects for the men neither. He had to agree. In no case whatever had Harry heard of a woman with four fucking husbands.

"What's to be signified by the hat?" Harry asked, "Other than your preacher is three bricks short of a load."

"The book of Mormon, Harry, was revealed to Joseph Smith by the angel Moroni, in the form of two golden tablets which he could decipher by putting the tablets into a tall hat, and using a special stone to translate them, while he dictated what he read to his friend, who scribed it for him."

"That's pure stupidity. If God had Himself a revelation to make, I reckon He'd make it personally. No fucking offense."

"His ways are mysterious," the Judge said, with that lecturing tone of his, "and it may be that we cannot behold his majesty direct, in the same way that to stare too long at the sun can render a man bereft of sight. I was once like you, Harry. Cold and directionless, angry and wild. I killed for sport and pleasure, but Esperanza brought me to God."

Harry walked away toward the tail end of that, not caring much for sermons, nor for any more of any of this. Yet the cat was out of the bag. He had to listen to it all day long, nodding and saying as little as he could get away with.

In turns, they told him of the glorious plan of God. As Harry pieced it together, it was like this: The Mormons believed that spirits go through phases of growth, and that what men are, God Himself once was. They believed that there were other creations with their own Gods, and that a righteous man (and, some believed, women) might ascend to become a God of their own creation through righteous behaviour and through the covenant of plural marriage and the creation of vessels for purified souls in the form of children. This put the ones who couldn't die in something of a bind. They couldn't die, or so it seemed, and so they seemed also to have no way of ascending.

It seemed, to them, further, that there was some similarity between the stories of the Stone and the Silver, and the of the golden tablets of Joseph Smith and of his Seer Stone. The plates were described as having words that flowed and bubbled on the surface like quicksilver. They felt sure that the Silver in their bodies was of the same stuff as the Golden Tablets. They were themselves some kind of revelation.

There were far fewer women who could not die, and a surplus of men. This was coupled with the fact that the stuff inside them had made them less fertile. No child had yet been conceived of two of the undying. It was decided that the women then should have many husbands to increase the possibility that they might produce a child. Such a rare and already divinely advanced child would surely be the rebirth of Jesus Christ Himself, come to lead the war on Armageddon with His Army of Undying Saints.

They were themselves the vessels for God's return, and would be His army on the day of Armageddon.

This was, of course, explained in dribs and drabs and parables, and with a lot of exaltations to the fucking lord, so Harry was sure he'd missed a lot of it. After a long and, to him, blessed silence, the sun was sinking down, and night was approaching.

"Am I understanding this right?" Harry finally said, "Are you asking me to fucking marry you?"

All of them laughed, even the Frenchie, and his laugh was as sharp as his eyes were cold.

"You ain't my type," Holden said.

"If the Prophet says so, then yes, we will ask you," Esperanza said.

"I thought he was the fucking prophet?" Harry aimed a thumb at the preacher.

"He's a prophet," she replied. "But he isn't THE Prophet."

"No matter what he thinks," Holden added. The preacher smiled sheepishly and shrugged his shoulders.

"And that's who we're riding to see?" he asked.

"Yep," Holden answered.

"Brigham Young?" Harry asked.

"Not that fool, that heretic pretender." Esperanza said with a bitter edge, "the true Prophet, Joseph Smith. Though the world does not know, he was one of the first in America to be saved."

Harry felt his stomach roll.

"Well, if that don't beat all," Harry said, and he meant it, though not with the genuine gladness he feigned. It rang true as he said it, a good sign. He was out of practice lying. "I reckon I've never met me a man who talked to an Angel before."

"You will have by this time next Saturday," Esperanza said.

No, Harry thought. I don't reckon I will.

That night he sang and even prayed with them, and listened to her fuck the priest, with him screaming Amen and Hallelujah through the act like a fucking simpleton. When they were all asleep, he went to his horse, and fetched his hatchet, a glass bottle of kerosene, and a box of matches.

He dealt with the Frenchie first, raising the hatchet and slicing down in one quick motion, taking the head clean off in one stroke. He had never been so glad to be so fucking strong. The eyes opened, and the mouth tried to scream, but it had no lungs to push air. He considered putting it into the embers but though the smell and smoke might rouse them. He kicked it into the water. The others were still asleep.

He didn't reckon he could cut through Holden's thick neck in one stroke. The god-forsaken fucker had muscles like wood. The preacher he could do, and he did, kicking it into the water likewise.

He straddled Holden's broad chest and took the hatchet in one hand, and the kerosene in the other. He raised the hatchet and cleaved it straight down into the man's forehead. The kerosene he poured straight in the wound and he hacked down again.

The Judge screamed, blinded by fumes, and striking out at him. Esperanza woke up screaming and confused. Harry leaped off of Holden's writhing blubbery body as he tried to stand and kept falling. Holden's gutsilver flashed and roiled in the gaping wound in the middle of his face. Esperanza saw Harry strike the first match and leaped at him with the ferocity of a bitch defending its pups. He shoved her down, one long gouge across his cheek from her painted nails, and the second match he tossed on the Judge. He went up like a lantern, his gutsilver overwhelmed, Harry saw it lurch back from the flames and into the charring bones as the Judge fell still.

Esperanza had the fight taken out of her, as she watched the Judge burn, as she saw the headless bodies of her other two husbands. Her eyes were wide with horror. He waited until the Judge went out, and kicked the head free of his spine. Even then, she didn't move.

He knelt down in front of her.

"We...we did nothing to you," she said.

"You know what," Harry said, "that's so. I had an inkling that you might not be inclined, actually, to let me go against the word of your fucking prophet once I got to Deseret. I took my chances here instead. You tell your prophet I ain't interested, and to stay the fuck away from me."

She looked at him through eyes glazed with tears.

"You butchered them," she said.

"They'll get better. I'm riding home. And lady, if you were for real, and you would have let me go, well...you're good Christians. Forgive me."

He rode back up the trail.

CHAPTER SIXTEEN

Green River Trail 1882

HARRY WAS ASLEEP, PARTLY IN the underbrush, to stay out of sight, and his horse tethered a little further into the trees. He had felt naked and alone on the road, and had been overcome with a bad feeling, and the feeling of being watched. Still, he was bone-tired after long day's ride, and still feeling half queasy from the violence of the night before. His sleep was fitful, and he was right to think he was being watched.

From high in the mountains, Bear-On-Fire had seen the gods and their quarrel. Not knowing what side was in the right, he stayed clear of it, troubled only by a strange familiarity about the blond god who rode off after shedding blood. He could see the whole day's ride from where he was, and some more. Less than two hours after the blond god left the woman weeping and alone, four more gods rode up to her. They had been riding to meet the ruined men on their way home. The group of them had then set out at once to catch up with the man who'd torn apart their companions. One man stayed behind to look for the heads of the men who'd been parted from them.

Bear-On-Fire could hear their tiny cries, tiny doll-like bodies growing at the stem of the torn neck, and he considered coming down to help, but what he'd heard of these white gods and their religion did not make him any more inclined to meet them.

And now, the white Mormon gods had caught up to the one who slept in hiding. There would be more fighting, but in the end, nobody here would be killed. He chose to do nothing and try to learn.

CHAPTER SEVENTEEN

Green River Trail 1882

HARRY WAS LIFTED TO HIS feet by two strong men, and as soon as his eyes adjusted to being awake, he saw Esperanza standing in front of him, and he knew for fucking certain that he was in for a world of suffering. He didn't know how she had caught up to him, or who these assholes were that were riding with her.

"You pig," she said to him, her eyes burning with a passion that made his skin crawl cold.

"Okay," Harry said, "Do what you have to, but can we skip the fuckin' sermon? I had my fill already."

The men pulled his shoulders out of their sockets and held him fast. The pain went through him, and his vision went grey on him. He could only whimper.

"You'll get no more sermon from me," she said. "We came to offer you salvation, and you paid us with violence. You have to atone in blood, and that's a shame for you, because it'll last forever. I'm going to leave you for Jules and the Judge."

"That's a relief," Harry said, trying to stay brave, "they're both sissies."

She slapped his face with her nails hooked in to tear four deep gouges in his face. He winced, but what was a little more pain at this point.

"You'll find out how very interested The Judge is in the nature of pain," she said. "It's his genius, through no fault of his own. Only he and Jules will be a while getting over the savagery you've done them. My husbands and I have to go now and see to them, and you can't be trusted to come along."

Harry had a moment's hope they meant to let him go after maiming him in some way, but knew deeper down there was no such mercy here. The other man had been standing in shadows, and he was holding what looked like six railroad spikes, but two feet longer than they should have been, three in each hand.

"We have ways of handling monsters like you. You're going to stay right here a while."

His eyes went wide as he understood the fullness of what they meant to do.

The two men held him to the ground, and Esperanza helped, sitting on his legs as the fourth man used a hammer to drive the spikes in at the shoulders and knees, one through the heart, and one through the pelvis. He screamed and jerked against them, but could not budge, and every motion caused further agony. Any attempt to move his arms made him near to pass out from it.

They cut off his hands and put them on his chest, and then Esperanza straddled his chest, and leaned down close to his sweating bug-eyed face, strained in rictus. He prayed for pain to stop, but it kept coming until he could no longer even draw air to scream. The stake through his heart burned, as the gutsilver tried again and again to heal what it could not fix, but he did not fade to blackness. She smiled at him, and nose to nose, she whispered, "We'll be back for you."

She pressed her long red thumbnails to his eyes and pressed in until they came back slick with gore. He screamed, and she packed his eyes with loose dirt.

The pain and the darkness was everything, and Harry believed in hell again.

CHAPTER EIGHTEEN

Green River Trail 1882

BEAR-ON-FIRE STOOD BESIDE the blond god, and his own mind was filled with the pain of him. He had not stood so close to another living person in ten summers or more. Had he chosen to, he might have leaned down and touched this man. He felt ill for the first time he could even remember, his stomach rebelled against the sight of this atrocity. He could feel the man's body screaming to repair itself, trying to work around the iron driven through it. The man's thoughts were empty of anything but the pure desire for an end to pain. He was not thinking of his regrets or of his woman, nor even of his mother as so many did when they suffered unto death. He thought of nothing but his own pain.

He did not know if this man was in the right, or if he was wrong. Certainly, he had done terrible things to the others, and this had been done to him in the name of vengeance. Vengeance was a concept he could understand. When he had watched this happen from his roosting place some miles away and above it, it had seemed easier somehow to stay apart from it. He knew that the wise thing to do was to walk away. He further knew he could not do the wise thing.

He knelt beside the man, and as gently as he could, he used the tip of the man's knife to take the earth from his eye sockets. The man screamed anew, his throat hoarse with pain, and trying to form words. As the largest part of the soil came free, the sockets seemed to fill with silver, and then he saw an eye regrow as though someone had poured it back in place. Soon the other eye was restored as well, and both were fixed on him. They were the brightest blue, like the sky without clouds. It was then he recognized the god as Harry Parker.

Sharply, he took in breath, and grasped the spike that pinned Harry to the earth through his pelvis, pulling it free as quickly as he could. Then he pulled the spike from his heart and, at once, felt it start to beat again. He heard air whistling into Harry's healing lung. He then considered which would be the proper order to most keep Harry's flailing to a minimum. He removed the spike from the left shoulder, and then the right knee.

As expected, Harry began to move, and each motion caused him further agony. Bear-On-Fire held him down and spoke softly.

"Try to be still," he said, words feeling strange in his mouth. "You will be free soon."

Harry nodded, looking at him with pure gratitude and closed his eyes to brace himself, as Bear-On-Fire pulled free the last two spikes. Harry curled himself into a ball and howled in his pain.

Bear-on-Fire wiped the spikes in the grass and set them in a pile, and watched as Harry rocked side to side. He sat at a respectful distance until the pain was over. It did not take long for the physical pain to stop, but Harry Parker had taken a wound to the soul. It would likely ache at night for as long as he lived.

Harry laid on his side, as his breath came to him, and then sat up slowly.

"Thank you," Harry said, "I owe you more than words can fuckin' tell you."

Bear-On-Fire nodded.

"You speak English?"

Bear-On-Fire nodded.

"Not a talker, eh?" Harry tried to stand, and fell back down to one knee. Bear-On-Fire was at his side in an instant to help him up. Harry put a hand on his shoulder and looked at him with some surprise and then took a step back. "Are you one of them?"

"The Mormons?" he answered, and Harry nodded. "No, but I am a god like you."

Harry threw his head back and laughed.

"Friend," he said, "If you're a god, which I doubt, you're nothing like me. I'm just a sinner with star muck in his veins. I'm a fucking accident."

Bear-On-Fire considered what Harry had said, and did not know, in the end, what to think.

"Where's my horse?" Harry asked, and headed to the brush. He turned back in a second, and had a look of real pain on his face. "They took him. Hell."

"I saw them go with him, to the west," Bear-On-Fire said.

"Better that than they shot him. Whatever the hell is wrong with them, and that's plenty, I don't reckon them for horse killers. Every Mormon I've known took care of their stock better than their children."

"I should...," Bear-On-Fire said, "I should go."

Harry cocked his head at him.

"Wait a second," he said, "You ain't no Indian are you? You look like a Chinaman."

Bear-On-Fire had seen a handful of these Chinamen, from far away, and had noted the resemblance. The language they had spoken to each other was familiar, but not, he'd thought, the language of his childhood.

"I fell from the sky in a stone," Bear-On-Fire said, "and was raised by the People to the north of here."

Harry smiled.

"Well, the Chinamen do call themselves Celestials, but I don't think I ever heard of them having no kingdom in the sky. You sure your people weren't sporting with you? Most every Indian I ever got to know had himself a teasing way."

Bear-On-Fire smiled back.

"I still remember when they found me," he said. "But you are right. It is a story they would make up."

"Well," Harry said. "Who the fuck am I to judge. I'm a fucking immortal, now, and the world is clearly full of all matter of unknowable crazy."

Harry picked his hat up off the ground, slapped it over his thighs, and placed it on his head. He then offered Bear-on-Fire his hand to shake.

"My name's Harry Parker," he said, "and you can believe you've got a loyal friend for life in me."

Bear-On-Fire felt tears spring to his eyes, and did all that he could do to keep them back. He wanted to seem strong and to be a man. He clasped Harry's forearm in his hand, and Harry squeezed his. In that moment, Bear-On-Fire knew that Harry was no more this man's real name than Bear-On-Fire was his. Both of them had taken new names on manhood, and both had been changed by them. Harry's memories came into him, and he saw that each of them had built their own loneliness.

"I am Xiao Le," he said, his voice tight.

"Well, Charley," Harry said. "It's a pleasure to have made your acquaintance."

The men released each other, and looked at each other in silence for a second.

"Well," Harry said, "It's a long walk back to Clanton, and I know you've got places to be. So I guess we'll part ways. If you're ever Clanton way, you ask for Harry Parker."

"I could walk with you a way," Xiao Le said.

"That'd be just fine with me," Harry said. "I ain't had much luck traveling on my own. I sure as hell can't stay here though. Those fuckers'll be back soon enough, and I'd rather they had to come all the way to Clanton where I can be ready for them."

"What will you do?"

"I...I don't rightly know what you do with a man you can't have around but can't kill. I reckon I'll come up with something. Maybe I'll get lucky, and when they find I'm gone, they'll call it square."

Xiao Le said nothing.

"Yeah," Harry said, "I know. It ain't likely."

"It is a nice dream though," Xiao Le said. "You should enjoy it for a while."

Harry clapped him on the back and laughed, and they began to walk together along the trail.

CHAPTER NINETEEN

Near Clanton Colorado 1882

THREE DAYS OF WALKING WAS, surprisingly, a considerable time to get to know a man. Charley, for a man who still seemed strange with words, had held up his end. They'd swapped their stories. Charley seemed taken by Harry's tales of his time in Mexico, and Charley had shared stories of what these lands had been like before the whites had come in droves. Charley was older than he looked, over a hundred-twenty summers from when his people had found him. From the things he said, they sounded like the Cree maybe. If there was anything in what the Mormons had said, then he was as old as any man on earth.

He had repeated the tale the Mormons had told him, about the Stone that landed near Africa, and how it formed the Salt Mouse Island, and how this whole ungodly mess of undying men had sprung up there. Charley had been taken aback by that, his face uneasy.

"It seems to me," he said at last, "that stone is my brother. Or my mother."

Harry cocked a head in his direction.

"I don't follow your meaning."

"The night the I fell to Earth the people say there was one great light in the sky, headed west. I fell in a smaller light that fell from the great one. The great one continued on far past seeing."

Harry whistled.

"That does," he said, "right enough seem no kind of coincidence."

They walked on. Charley looked like a man straining to keep his pace slow. Harry had the sense that, left to his own pace, Charley'd have been in Clanton pretty much ten minutes after setting off. He wasn't sure just what kept Charley with him, but he was damned grateful.

"If they were not such crazy white people," Charley said, "I'd have questions for them."

"If it makes you feel any better Charley, I think they made up most of what else they think they know."

Charley nodded, not so much in agreement as in acknowledgement.

"Some day I would like to go to that Salt Mouse Island," Charley said. "I hope it will be the first land I have known with more answers than questions."

"I wouldn't count on it, Charley. This world seems designed to fucking confound."

"That's true," Charley said.

"Well," Harry said, "Once this present situation is resolved, we'll find that Salt Mouse Island, you and me. I got only the vaguest fucking idea where it is, but folks like us, we got nothing but time."

"You would do that?"

"Sure, I would. I got some questions of my own, and who wouldn't. Mostly though, you're my friend, and if you want to go there, I am fucking going to help you."

"It will not be easy, whether I am seen as a red man or a Chinaman. White men will not like that we are friends."

"Fuck those people," Harry said. "They're half of them fucking stone ignorant, and the other half wicked. I'll knock down any man who so much as looks at you crosswise."

Charley's eyes seemed grateful in a way that made him feel pure shame for the way his people had behaved in this new world. It wasn't the first time, and that shame was part of what drove him to drink, and to Clanton, and his jailhouse.

"Your enemies are my enemies, too, Harry. They will have to kill me as well."

"Well, all right," Harry said.

Charley put a hand on his shoulder, his hand as heavy as a bar of gold, his strength controlled by a powerful gentleness. He stopped Harry from walking.

"My people have a..." Charley struggled for the word in English, then shrugged and gave up, "... a thing we do when we take a man as a brother. Would you do this thing with me?"

Harry swallowed.

"Reckon I'd be honoured."

Charley produced a knife from his breeches, and ran the blade across his hand, the wound already starting to close as the knife was done. Harry took the knife and did the same as Charley nodded. They clasped hands quickly, sharing blood and silver. Harry could feel the other man's silver in his wound, moving and healing. Their hands had healed together as one flesh. Each could see the surprise in the other man's eyes. They held like this for some time as one joined man, their blood flowing one to the other.

"My blood and yours," Charley said. "One blood."

"Reckon so," Harry said, solemnly, then smiled. "This is going to hurt like a bitch when we let go."

"It should," Charley said.

They pulled their hands back, and the pain was as bad as Harry had figured on. He didn't mind. It was a whisper compared to the ordeals of a few days past. This was a different pain, in any case. It was the pain of a new start. He'd seen women give birth, and he knew that no soul had ever come born anew without a profuse pain, and some considerable struggle.

They didn't need to talk for most of that day. Just before the sun set, they saw the lanterns in the windows of Clanton.

CHAPTER TWENTY

Clanton, Colorado 1883

WINTER HAD SETTLED IN, AND so had the new year. Xiao Le had seen his first Christmas in town. He had gone to the big church supper, and been treated with kindness and decency. This was, in part, because, on their arrival in the autumn, Harry had beaten bloody the first six men who had treated him as less than his brother. There had not been a seventh man brave enough. Since then, Xiao Le had done his best to prove his worth, lending his strong arms to help with harvest, and taking work for pay. He had restrained himself enough that, while no man would question his effort, he would not draw awe or suspicion. He had begun to enjoy the company of people again.

The townspeople had been grateful to him as well, for Harry had changed since their return. He talked with his neighbours, and joked with them. He was no less likely to curse, but he made, at least, an effort to civility, and tried to keep his tongue civil in the company of women.

Xiao Le was clearing the snow from the wooden walkway out front of the jail house with a shovel when Kenneth Jones walked by.

"Good morning, Enkidu," Smith said, tipping his hat.

"Morning," Xiao Le answered, half a frown on his face.

"Is our Gilgamesh about?" Jones asked, a broad smile beneath his red handlebar moustaches, waxed finely at the tips. Harry called him the Walrus, and had shown Xiao Le a drawing of such a creature. The similarity in size and face was considerable.

"Do you mean Harry?"

"I do," Jones answered. "I'm sorry. I only mean to imply that you've gentled down our Marshall considerably. Your influence upon his temperament has been highly beneficial to him, to all of us. He's a finer man when sober than ever when he was drinking."

Xiao Le didn't understand exactly what Jones was referring to, but understood his meaning somewhat.

"Harry is at the saloon," Xiao Le said. "But not drinking."

"Well, I'll seek him out there. Thank you."

Xiao Le nodded as Jones waddled his way to the saloon. It made him glad to be a part of things. He felt human in a way he had not since he took his name. He enjoyed shovelling snow. It was simple work, but when he was done he could look at it, and see what he'd done. Once he'd finished the walk before the jailhouse, he proceeded to shovel the remainder of the boardwalk along both sides of the street. When it was done, he had worked up a mild sweat, and it felt good.

Harry found him, sitting on a stool just outside the door to the jailhouse. Harry's face was pale, and his hands were shaking. Xiao Le stood up, and did not need to say any words to ask what was wrong.

"Trouble is coming in the spring, Charley. Worse than I ever guessed. Jones just told me that there's Mormon trouble. They say there's a small army of Mormons just across the border. He reckons it's a show of force, intended to shy back the government a bit on the issue of statehood for Utah. I reckon differently."

Xiao Le was not afraid. What use was fear to a man who couldn't die? He had never seen any man, or any god, who could restrain him against his will. He would not suffer the fates he'd seen. His concern was for Harry. Harry was stronger than a normal man, and his reflexes fast. When distracted or tired, Harry's hearing seemed to become strong, or he started to see into men's minds, but he seemed only half aware of that. He was not mighty. He was the equal, perhaps, of one of these Mormon gods, but could be easily overwhelmed.

He was without any doubt that he could restrain many, or possibly all, of these men but, unless the fight were in private, he dared not use his full powers. If he did use them, then nothing in this town would be the same for him, or for Harry. He feared that even Harry would feel differently about him if he truly saw the strength that Xiao Le possessed.

"They will be coming for you," he said. "They will be surprised to see me with you."

"Well, that's true, but it's still two men against God knows how many."

"We will win, Harry, for all the gods are on our side, and because we are good men."

"Christ, Charley. Save that for some other son of a bitch who never saw a shooting war."

"I promise you it will be as I say, Harry. Have I ever said something that wasn't true?"

"Not a lie, no. You did say you were a god fallen from the sky, though, so I reckon you're as capable of being wrong as the next man."

"Not when the next man is you, white man."

Xiao Le smiled and Harry smiled back.

"There are good people in this town gonna get hurt. I'm scared worse than ever before in all my life," Harry said, meaning it, and still smiling.

"That's because you value life," Xiao Le said. "I'd call it a blessing."

"I ain't had a fucking drink since we met. I don't know fucking why or how that works, but I'm thinking I might have a nip just now."

"Will that kill your fear?"

"No," he said, "but I reckon it'll make me mean enough to stand it."

Xiao Le stood up.

"If you want to drink, then do it with your friends. And leave your guns with me."

Harry unstrapped his gun belt and laid it in Xiao Le's arms. It was the first time in ten years that he'd taken it off for longer than it took to change his clothes, or take a bath. He'd slept with it on most nights. It felt weird, and he felt too light without it.

"If some son of a bitch in there takes his chance to shoot me," Harry said, "I'm coming back here to bloody your nose."

Xiao Le laughed, and Harry walked to the saloon. Xiao Le sat back down, holding his friend's gun for him, and leaned his head back, the cold not bitter, and took a nap.

CHAPTER TWENTY-ONE

Clanton Colorado 1883

INDIANS MADE FAMOUSLY GOOD SCOUTS, and Charley was the best Harry had ever seen. The moment winter had broken and travel made any kind of sense, Charley'd taken to finding high ground and watching the town. It'd been all clear so far. Every day Harry would check in with Jones to see if there had been any news by wire. This had been their habit for two weeks.

Harry and Charley had come up with a plan of sorts, and it was just a matter of doing it now. It would work, or it wouldn't. One way or the other, there'd be some kind of a resolution to the situation. There was no place he could run to that they wouldn't try to find him. If he ran, chances were they'd take it out on his town. He had no earthly choice but to make his stand and, if need be, take his licks for the next thousand years.

It was Wednesday, the third week of March when the newspaper man rushed to Harry's jailhouse. His face was red and sweaty. He'd run the distance from his place of business. It wasn't a long run, but he was a big man, and unaccustomed to physical work.

"Harry," the man said, "the Mormons have crossed the border. Most of them are headed south of Clanton, but the report says that some part of their number are headed this way."

He paused to catch his breath, and to mop his forehead with a linen handkerchief.

"Should I telegraph for assistance, Harry? The Sheriff?"

Harry shook his head, and took a breath.

"Sheriff is gonna be plenty busy trying to deal with the ones headed south, and trying to call for help from the Federal government, for all the good that'll do. I reckon that, as fucking usual, we're on our own."

The Walrus looked shaken and hesitant, but he nodded.

"And for the love of god, keep this to your fucking self, or else the Mormons we have right here in town are gonna wind up lynched or wonder if they need to switch sides. If I have my way, I'll turn these fuckers back before they ever hit town."

"With all due respect, Mr. Parker," he said, in an unusual display of gumption. "You and your deputy are two men, and they are coming in force. As formidable as your talents are, I fear that you may be overconfident."

"Well, Mr. Jones," said Harry, "I'll let you in on a little secret. Do I have your word?"

As he nodded, the Walrus' moustaches bobbled comically.

"Charley and I won't be alone out there. He has fetched some of his tribe up into the woods near here. These are Mormons coming, and they're none of them trained fighters. Charley and his kin, on the other hand have some experience in these matters. Rest easy. I reckon our numbers'll be about even."

The Walrus seemed to relax a little, although it might have been his breath starting to return to him after his running over.

"Oh," he said, "I see. Yes, I see. May I ask why you haven't tried to raise men amongst the locals?"

"Didn't see the need. Planting to be done."

"All right then," the Walrus said, seeming to be put to some ease by Harry's casual way about the matter. "I'll keep it under my hat until you deem otherwise, as a matter of courtesy. I trust you'll favour me with a first hand account of the conflict should there be one?"

"Oh hell," Harry said, "Who else would even listen to me? It ain't hardly gonna be anything worth speaking about. These are Mormons. Fuckers don't even know how to cuss properly. Don't drink coffee. We catch em in the early morning, and they'll be in Utah by noon."

"Well," Jones said, "I do pray you're right.

He waddled back toward his offices and his press. Harry sat back in his chair and let out a breath. He was ashamed at having learned so well to lie. He looked at his Peacemaker, holding it in his hand. He'd had this gun since before becoming marshall. It wasn't as pretty as that fucking antique he'd ridden out of Sill Creek with, four wet barrels, and still using ball and cap, but it was a sight more useful. Metal cartridge ammunition, a true wheelgun. Easy to use, and easy to reload, and tit useless against the riders headed to drag him to a thousand years of torture, if need be, until they broke his spirit, probably, and turned him to their sick religion.

His father had taught him that violence was no fit solution to any problem, and he'd turned his back on that. For a long time he'd forgotten any way to parley at all. Now, he wished urgently that this matter could be settled with a conversation. The Mormons had vengeance on their minds, and he had to admit he had some measure of desire for the same. He despised the wickedness of the human spirit, and didn't need any God to tell him it was rotten. If he'd felt he could reason with these people, he'd not have done such violence in his escape. He'd wanted to do more than buy freedom, he had hoped to terrify.

These people didn't scare easy. Mormons had set up the beehive as the symbol for their Deseret, and he had sure enough stuck a stick into that hive, and now they meant to sting him, had to. They had no more choice in their minds than he'd had in his when he set the Judge afire.

So, this was going to be a fight, he reckoned, in which you could see the side of both parties. That was usually the way. On the other hand, he also allowed, one half of this fight was a single lawman who never asked to be involved, and the other party was a pack of lunatics courting Armageddon and practicing unholy fornication in the name of God. He reckoned his sympathies as belonging to him, even once he tried to step back a bit.

On the road, half a mile out of town, was Clanton Stables. It was no longer in use. The proprietor had decided a year or two back that the business was not profitable. He'd headed south for Arizona and left the buildings where they stood. He'd never rightly owned the land, and nobody else had stepped in to use the buildings yet, except as spare timber. Folk often snuck out here to "borrow" a plank or two. The buildings now looked abandoned and the land had slowly started to reclaim them. It was there that Harry and Charley had decided to make their stand. Their plan would involve some horses getting hurt. He didn't love that, but it seemed the only plan that made sense.

An hour after the Walrus had left, Charley came into the jailhouse.

"See anything?" he asked his friend.

Charley nodded.

"Fifteen men. Two women," Charley said. "A day or so up the trail."

Harry was willing to bet that one of those women was the Mexican bitch who'd clawed his eyes out for him. He would not make the mistake of sparing her for being a lady this time around. He was a drunk and a killer and a poor poet, but he did not reckon that he was a fool. He nodded at Charley.

"Yeah," he said, "The Walrus said that the Mormons had crossed the border, and that they had seen a smaller party split off this way. I reckon it's time. Told the Walrus that we'd called in help from your Tribe."

"Did he believe you?"

"How the fuck should I know? I did my best to lie."

"You could ask them to stand with us," he said. "Some would."

"I fuckin' know that, but I ain't risking the lives of people who die from bullets in a gunfight with people who don't."

"We won't need them, anyway."

"So you say. Let's get out there, we have a lot of fucking work to do."

They rode out of town together. The Walrus watched them go, and so did some of the others. Harry paid them no mind, as though this were a matter of the least possible concern.

They worked straight through the night with shovels, digging pits in the road. In those pits, they stuck in sharpened spikes of wood. Wouldn't kill these men to fall on them, but it would kill the horses, and they'd have a hell of a time pulling themselves off such a thing. Charley was fearsomely strong and quick, and it took the two of them no time at all to dig two such pits seven feet deep and five across. The poles they had carved out weeks ago and had left them in one of the stable houses. Likewise the canvas tarps they stretched out, and nailed down, and covered with dirt until you might not notice them at all.

Harry had been taken by a terrible fear that some wagon would come through town and straight onto the pits, and so, from that point on, either he or Charley kept half an eye on the them. They'd come to the decision that guns were of limited usefulness, and would only draw attention. Instead they had bought about twenty six-foot lengths of rod steel from the blacksmith and hammered one end of each of them to the best point they could manage. They weren't throwing spears, but they were designed to skewer a man and keep him at a distance.

Their best hope for success was that several of them would end up gored in the pits. While the party was caught off their guard by the pit trap, Harry was going to bombard them, throwing cow bladders filled nearly to bursting with lamp oil. Charley was to then start throwing lit bottles of fuel. No matter how calm a man was under pressure, being on fire interfered with strategic thinking.

That, he reckoned would even the odds somewhat. This all hinged on the fact these crazy bastards didn't think Harry had a friend in the world. He was gladder than hell that they were wrong.

CHAPTER TWENTY-TWO

Clanton, Colorado 1883

JUST AS DAWN ROSE, THE riders off a distance yet, Xiao Le excused himself to walk a while. He moved with swiftness into the forest and sat there, his eyes shut to clear his mind, and to pray to his gods for help. He sang low and soft, songs he'd learned as a boy. He smelled burning bear grease thick in his nose, and opened his eyes. His shadow, pointed away from the rising sun was sitting up, long black arms supporting its weight, and then it stood up, looking down at him, and he looked back.

"Is this my last morning, then?" Xiao Le asked. "Is this fight my destiny?"

The shadow shook it's head side to side.

"It's just a fight. Your destiny wakes when the island does."

"Why have you come?"

"You called on me because you are afraid. Why?"

"If we lose this fight, I lose Harry. He's my only friend."

"If that's so, then do not lose."

Xiao Le laughed.

"We won't," he said, "Our plan is strong, and it should work."

"It's a good plan," the shadow said, "but it's only a plan."

The shadow faded away as it had the first time. Xiao Le was left with his thoughts.

The choice between two fears was always hard. He knew that the choice between keeping Harry's easy affection, and keeping Harry well and walking was no real choice. If he was forced, he would show all of the powers at his command. Harry was his friend. Acting human was only a game Xiao Le had come to enjoy.

CHAPTER TWENTY-THREE

The Gunfight at Clanton Stables

WHEN CHARLEY CAME BACK, HE looked damned serious. Then he stopped, staring off toward the town with a grim smile. Harry looked at him with a cocked eyebrow.

"You make your fuckin' peace with your heathen gods?" he said, smiling.

"Yes. Harry. Never forget I am your brother. Whatever should happen in this fight, remember that I am Charley, and that I am your friend."

"Aw hell, don't get sentimental on me now. I can't afford to start in with crying. Hard to fight with puffy eyes, and all."

Charley nodded, and forced a little smile before heading into his position of cover, where his bottles were ready for use, and his share of the makeshift pole-arms. When his back turned, Harry spoke.

"Reckon I love you too, you ignorant savage," Harry said, still mocking his friend, but meaning it, and meaning it to come across like he did.

Harry crouched low, taking cover behind rotted planks that he'd earlier leaned against the fence. He could peer out through a tiny gap in the wood. He had a clear view of the road. They each stayed in their hiding spots, trying to remain silent. It was boring and awkward and went on for a lot longer than Harry cared for, but if any of the others had a sense of hearing like Charley, it still wouldn't be enough. Smell was an issue too. He could still smell the kerosene in his makeshift balloons, and he was worried that some canny fucker in their party would smell it too.

He could hear them, then, coming in from the West. They were singing fucking hymns, with no fear of being heard whatsoever. The singing got louder as they drew closer. Harry felt something very like anticipation in their approach. The best plan in the world only worked half as good as you hoped, and he could only even pray that he walked away from this.

His attention was entirely focused on the road, and for the first glimpse of the ones who'd come for him. It was as though the rest of the world had faded away. He knew, knew in his bones, that Esperanza would be the fucking first to come around that little twist in the road, with her mad zealot fucking eyes, and a funeral flower in her hair.

His surprise was total when the first one around the bend was a thin brown haired pansy-looking sort with a beak on him like an eagle. Two more rode behind him at a respectful distance, as though he were the leader of the lot of them. Behind those two were Esperanza and her fucking man-harem. Holden, the Preacher and Frenchie all looked as good as new, but grim. The other fuckers that had nailed him to the ground were there too, and the rest he did not know. The horses seemed a bit nervous, the singing had stopped.

He realized then, that he was looking at Joseph Smith, supposedly torn to pieces by a crowd thirty years ago for his fucking heretic beliefs, but now clearly alive and as batshit crazy as he ever was. Harry had seen enough drawings of the man to recognize him. Esmerelda had told him that they would meet, but Harry had assumed that to be horse shit.

He held his breath and then he heard the sound of a horse screaming. Smith's horse faltered as its hoof came down on canvas instead of hard ground, and stumbled. The horse to its right plunged straight into the pit trap and so did the rider. Smith too, pitched forward and landed up in the pit. His howling, and the howling of the horses was terrible. The remaining horses reared and spooked. It wasn't as many bodies as he wanted to see go in, but the distraction was perfect.

He lobbed balloon after balloon at the flock of them, and could see them bursting. He could smell the heavy, greasy smell of the fuel. Exposed, he stood up and kept lobbing as the first lit bottle flew into the midst of them. The fire spread onto the road, and caught on anything Harry'd splashed with fuel. The chaos was near total, and the smell and scream of burning men and horses was, he imagined, a foretaste of the noises and smells in hell.

He took, in both hands, one of the sharpened iron rods and rushed one of the men currently running around like an axe-struck chicken. Another was trampled as a horse ran from the fire, flanks aflame, off into the woods. He caught the man in the chest, the fucker practically running himself up on the and braced it against his hip and shoved him over into the pit. He slid wetly off the rod and into the hole, where he landed up on a stake, writhing with his prophet and with his own horse. Harry pulled his gun, and shot the horse once in the head, ending its suffering quick.

Charley was dealing similar agonies to another man as Harry turned to look. That was when the shot rang out from behind him, and one of the Mormons took it in the back just as he'd got his horse away from the fire, near settled. Harry wheeled and saw a posse of townsfolk. Amongst their number was Ellie McCabe with her father's shotgun, and the Walrus himself. The Walrus raised his own rifle in salute.

"You're a god-awful terrible liar, Mr. Parker," the Walrus shouted, and Harry wanted to punch him in his face.

Ellie was looking at him with a smug, "I told you so" smile, which both vexed him and made her look adorable as a new-born baby. He was touched and terrified all at once. These people who had come out of loyalty and affection to him, god knows why, were like kittens in the path of an angry Grizzly, and didn't know it.

Something like half of the Mormons were laying on the road, burned past any ability to be of use at the moment, or in the pit, in pure agony. The rest had taken cover in the trees that lined the trail. He could hear them whispering. They could hear their Prophet still moaning on his stake.

He and Charley looked at each other and the townsfolk took their cover in the stables, guns levelled at the woods.

"Pull the Prophet off the stake," Esperanza shouted from cover, "and we can talk."

"Not fucking likely," Harry said, as the last of the fuel on the road burned out. He shot two more horses in the skull and stopped their moaning. The rest had run off or been dispatched by the other side.

Charley stood with another spear in his hands, watching the bush carefully.

"Did you fuckin' know they were coming?" Harry said to him, cocking his head to the self-appointed deputies.

Charley nodded.

"A man should have the right to fight if he chooses."

"If we get out of this," Harry said, "I'm going to whup you."

"You can try," Charley said.

"Take your fucking people, and leave," Harry shouted. "I'll let you go, if you go now. Once I see you going, I'll pull your Prophet off the stake and send him back your way. You have my word."

"Fuck your word, you back-shooting cocksucker," came another voice, Holden's, he thought.

"Oh did you come along for some more, Judge?"

"You know I fucking did."

Harry kicked a burned man over that he reckoned was the Preacher, or would be once he healed up. He lifted his boot and cracked it down on the skull.

"You're right, it is nice that I get to do it to you more'n once!" Harry shouted to the Judge who fairly growled.

"What's the matter, white men?" Charley shouted. "Why don't you come for us? Are you scared of two men against all of you, or is it the guns that scare you? Do you fear a little pain?"

"Fuck you, savage!" Esperanza shouted.

Harry fired a shot off in the direction of her voice, and there was a wounded yell that sounded like it came from a man.

"Oh, did I wing someone there, partner? Well, you're a good Christian. Forgive me."

Esperanza screamed and ran forward, the Judge and Frenchie at her side. Her eyes were maddened, and her nails were outstretched as she closed the distance for Harry. The Judge held a twenty pound hammer like it was a children's toy, and the Frenchie had a pigsticker that was probably, technically, a sword.

Harry braced his spear for the first one to come near, but the Judge swatted it aside like it was a twig with one hand and swung hard with the hammer. He felt his own teeth crack and splinter, and his jaw shattered like glass, and teeth flew like bloody raindrops. The pain was incredible, and he fell to the dirt with a jarring impact that re-aggravated the agony. Shots rang out from behind him, and were returned from cover by the other Mormons, and he heard a man behind him catch a shot. He also heard Esperanza scream.

The hammer was up above the Judge's head, fixing to slam down again on him, as Ellie screamed out loud.

"He's killed the marshall!" she shouted, stating what only seemed to be true, as she fired. The blast peppered the Judge across the chest, distracting him enough for Harry to roll on his back and get a real good look at that hammer as his face knitted itself up, and the business end of it started to drop.

Harry had been about ready to close his eyes and brace for fresh horror, when the Judge was knocked off his feet. Harry rolled to his side to see Charley grab the Judge by his head, and pull it clean off like he was pulling the head off a daisy. The head went into the pit. Charley took two shots in the back, which seemed to pain him, but only slow him. He turned to look at the Mormons firing, his eyes narrowed.

Harry sat up, to the gasps of the townsfolk behind him. Many were so startled they stopped firing. There was another scream, and he turned to see The Walrus take a bullet to the skull. His head blew apart and he slumped over, dead.

Esperanza and the Frenchie were now impaled on the same length of iron, moaning and staggering, trying to pull free. He tried not to enjoy the pain on their faces. When it became apparent that Frenchie was about to pull himself free, Harry put the barrel of his gun against his sweating forehead and pulled the trigger. His head exploded, and his limbs went still. He pulled the body off the stake the rest of the way, and rolled him into the pit, where, a few minutes later, having healed, his screaming began again from the flames, burning fuel having run off the road in sufficient quantity that the flames still burned in the pit, wooden stakes having taken to fire as well.

The last of the Mormons had advanced in a line from cover now, and they were shooting strictly at the townsfolk. Three of the burned bodies were stirring and trying to stand, pink skin under the ash, their burns maybe less serious than he'd previously imagined. That was terrible news for the outcome of the day.

Charley advanced on the Mormons, each shot causing him to cry out and hesitate. Harry fired a shot at the hand of one of the gunman, missed, catching a tree behind him. His last shot, as he reckoned.

He ran for the advancing line himself, gun in one hand, his knife in the other. Charley grabbed a man and pulled him in half. Harry saw it from the corner of his eye and also saw Charley take a shot in the face with a shotgun from about touching distance. He fell as seemingly stone dead as any man. Even though he knew it wasn't a killing blow to a man like Charley, that was his only fucking friend in this life, and he reacted accordingly. He screamed and pointed his gun on instinct, and he pulled the trigger on an empty chamber swearing at himself as he felt the bite of a knife into his ribs.

He then experienced for the first time the strangest feeling he'd had in a life full of the strange.

He twisted his gun back into the face of the woman who had just stabbed him, the last of their fucking queen bees, he realized, somehow just KNOWING, with a strange calm. As he pulled the trigger, he felt a cold tingling pleasurable rush through his arm. It felt as though he'd slept on the hand, and it was returning to life from being long asleep. There was a crack as loud as any he had ever heard, louder than any gunshot on earth. He could see the thing leave the barrel of his gun. It was a bullet of purest silver, torn from his own veins. It went into the forehead of the woman, and he felt her die, the silver in her bones dying or going to rust. When she fell, she would not be getting up. Something in him had destroyed something in her.

He heard the sound, then, of screaming as Ellie fell from a gunshot. The rest of the townsfolk were on their horses and riding for town, looking back over their shoulders. One horse reared, still panicked by his silver shot, and then carried on.

Another man closed on him, and he fired three silver bullets into his chest. The shots felt like hammer blows to his own sternum. Charley gasped in a lungful of air, Harry somehow hearing it in the chaos, and to see him back in the world calmed Harry considerably.

The Mormons closed on him, and he lay on his back firing again and again at them in turn. Charley plunged ahead, his face still a mask of gore, and pulled them back at sufficient pace so that Harry could keep firing. He lost count of how many times he was stabbed and kicked, and how many times he'd fired his gun. It all happened with a fierce quickness, though time often slowed in moments like this while you were in them. It was only in retrospect that he understood that none of them had had time to realize he was killing them for good, that their friends weren't getting back up.

The advance stopped, and he and Charley stood next to six dead men who could not, supposedly, die. Charley helped him to his feet and embraced him openly, the two of them holding each other up and feeling the hot breath of the other on his cheek.

"Now," Charley said, "we learn your real talent."

Harry pulled back.

"You should talk! I might've planned things a mite differently had I known that you could pull a man apart like a fucking cooked rabbit."

Charley laughed roughly, and heard the moaning of the burned men getting up.

"Oh, Hell no," Harry said, and one at a time, he dispatched them all.

He then turned to Esperanza who looked up at him with pleading eyes.

"Just couldn't take no for a fucking answer, could you, you snaky bitch?"

He put three bullets in her chest. She died with a sneer on her face.

There was still a handful of piteous fucking screams in the pit trap, but he was more concerned by the whimpering he heard down behind where the townsfolk had made their stand.

He ran behind the wall. All the men still there were dead. Ellie was still breathing, but with a small hole in her belly, and one in her back the size of his fist. Her eyes were glassy and agonized. He stared at her, paralyzed. He'd seen this girl all but grow up before his eyes. He'd seen her decency and her bravery. She'd had the grit to face him down in the name of brotherly love when every other human being in Clanton was too terrified to look at him. She was, in every way, the child that his own parents should have had in his place. She was sitting in her own blood and guts as the result of her own decency. He knew he was a monster, but he couldn't let her die for that. He decided to take it as an article of faith that she might do better than he had.

He took up a knife up from one of the dead, and cut deep into his arm. He pulled the gutsilver in handfuls as they sluggishly came and smeared it on her nose, her half open mouth, and it slid inside her. He was near to certain that he'd committed a mortal fucking sin in the name of this mercy.

In a minute, her eyes calmed, and she blinked, and then stared at him.

"I don't reckon you'll remember this all too clear, but I got three things to say before you nod off on me. One is thank you. The second is I'm fucking sorry, but I couldn't have your death on it, but I reckon I can live with having your life on my soul. The last is, stay away from other people with the silver if you can. Stay human as you can."

She looked confused, and shook her head side to side, She mumbled his name before her eyes closed, and she began to breathe deeply, and, eventually, fell to sleeping. She'd live a long time for what it was worth.

Which, he reckoned was either something, or no consolation at all depending on your viewpoint.

Charley stared at him.

"Did you give her the silver?" he asked, with a faint whiff of judgement in his voice.

"What would you have fuckin' done?" Harry said defensively.

"I don't know," Charley said.

"Well, then."

Harry stood back up, and the two of them walked back to the pit. Smith was on his stake. Another on his own. Two more were stuck on the iron rods. Harry had no recollection who had put them there. Charley probably. Holden and Frenchie's heads were staring up at him with the ragged stumps of their necks twitching and pulsing with the silver.

He shot Holden first because, if any one of them was going to be trouble, it would be him. Then he did for Frenchie, and the two on the rods, the one on the stake. That left Joseph Smith.

He looked Smith in the eyes, and Smith pleaded silently, with his hands clasped in front of him for mercy. Harry had no mercy for these cocksuckers. He couldn't afford it. Though he'd been born a Friend, and raised in the ways of peace, it wasn't his fault that God had given him a Concern in contradiction to that. His Concern, his one true work, was Death. The dealing of it to those who could not die was a mercy to some, justice to others, and something the world needed as much as the air itself. From this point on, he was the Law.

He smiled at Smith.

"Hey, Smith," he said, "Ever occur to you that your angel Moroni mighta just been a fucking dago in a blonde wig?"

And then he sent the man to meet his God, purified or no.

CHAPTER TWENTY-FOUR

Clanton and the Road

ONCE THE KILLING HAD BEEN done, Harry and Charley went back into town. Harry left his star on the desk, and packed up what he owned. He and Charley walked to the livery, as the townsfolk swamped them with questions. Halfway there, Harry stopped and raised a hand.

"Shut up for a goddamned minute," he shouted, "and I'll tell you what happened."

They looked at him with expectant eyes, and some of them with hero worship.

"A bunch of Mormons showed up, and Charley and I killed them. Some your friends and kin showed up and got themselves killed after I fucking told them not to. They're still out to the stables."

Some of the crowd dispersed at once to head out there.

"It's over now," Harry continued. "And me, I've had enough of law work. Reckon Charley and I are hitting the road. Now stand aside and let me go."

They looked at him, and their faces fell, but they parted for him. He paid for two horses in gold coins, of which he had a considerable supply from his times as a thief and a killer for hire. He'd refrained from spending them out of some sense of contrition, he supposed.

He and Charley rode east. There was no sense in trying to catch a train, though he could surely afford it, particularly once they'd dug up his cache of gold outside of town. The railways didn't let Indians ride except in cargo cars, nor Chinamen neither. It seemed they were good enough to build them, but not enough to ride. It was a beautiful god-damned country on horseback, anyhow.

They decided to ride east until they hit water and, once there, they'd sell the horses and find their way to England. He had questions needed answering, and so did Charley. Dorian-fancy-pants-Gray was an Englishman. It was a place to start.

There were, in the meantime, worse places to be than the open land on the back of a horse, and worse men to be with than the man who rode with him.

The world being the world, and Harry being the kind of man he was, of course, it was many many years before he saw England, and approximately a hundred and ninety injuries that would have killed a normal man.

As far as the world knew, Arise-Ye-Sons-Of-Israel Parker had likely died back in that gunfight, and he was just fine with that. It was freeing to be born again, as this instrument of higher law. He'd be keeping his eyes peeled for immortal cocksuckers in need of a killing. Seemed he had himself a calling.

CHAPTER TWENTY-FIVE

Edmonton, Alberta 2008

HARRY STOPS SHORT, AND RUBS the side of his head. He looks down at the book that has been tossed at him. It happened so quickly, I'd missed it.

"Goddamn your bones, you filthy savage," Harry says to the ancient man under his blanket.

"You talk too much, and you talk too loud, white man," Charley says, "I'm trying to sleep."

"Fine," Harry says, then looks back at me, "FOYNE."

"I beg your pardon," I say, the politeness in my voice straining, "what happened next?"

"Well, hell, all kinds of things."

"Look," I say, "I do have some questions that I don't just want answers to. I need them."

Harry nods, stands up and picks up a Stetson from the dining room table. It's white, of course.

"Let's walk a spell, and let the old man have his sleep."

I rise, and he and I head out the back door. His yard is wild, and untended, a little piece of what the land must have looked like before the settlers. There's a carriage house, and a back gate we walk through, turning down an alley. He looks at me, and smiles.

"Shoot," he says.

"Well first off, how many more have you had to kill?"

"Mortal or Immortal?" Harry asks.

"I suppose I don't know," I said, the question not having fully formed in me.

"Well," he said, "A considerable number of both. But more mortal than not. You got to understand, those were different times though. We undying cocksuckers have gotten civilized since then. We have judges now who set sentences and sometimes prison is all that we do. Longer sentences, but that's all. Mr. Gray, for example, is still alive as I hear it. He found God or some such and is living contritely."

"I see."

"What else?"

"Did you ever make it to the island? What happened? I need to know because, well, it's a long story, but whatever happened to me, and Christ if I even know honestly what DID happen, came about because of that same island. I probably should have guessed."

"Or Holmes should have told you."

"Yeah, or that."

"Well, most of what happened there is mighty personal, no offense. Let's just say that it was fucking terrible, and Charley's still recovering."

I didn't want to talk about the island either. Every time I did, I got a headache and a deeper sense of the numinous than I was comfortable with.

"Is he going to be okay?" I ask.

"He says he will. He's usually right. He sleeps all the time, the last forty years or so. Says he's tired. Time don't mean so much, and I ain't lonely. As you can see, has a way of making his fuckin' presence known. He says he'll wake up when the Island does, whatever the hell that means."

My stomach flips. I have a sense of unpleasant deja vu.

I nod. "My ex sometimes says the same thing in his sleep."

We've walked halfway around the block, now, and my stomach still hurts. Harry is quiet for a moment.

"Time don't mean much," Harry says quietly, "If you play the hand you're dealt."

I take his meaning straight to heart, and nod again.

"Well," Harry says as we make it to the walk out front of his house. "It's been a shorter visit than I expected, but I reckon as you know the rules, and I think you know everything I've got to teach you."

I shake his hand, too full of thought to speak, and he doesn't seem fussed by it.

"Listen," I say, thinking hard about my ex, laying in his hospital bed across an ocean, blind and mad, and waiting for the island to awaken. I feel small and disconnected, and alone. Really fucking alone, and maybe, just maybe, tired of it. "Do you think we might talk again sometime. I don't have a lot of friends, and you're really interesting. Christ. Why not just say, do you want to be my friend like we're five."

I shake my head feeling small and silly.

"Hell," he says, "Sure we can be pals. Got nothing but time. I like the sound of your voice, and you got a brain on you. Reckon you can drop by anytime you like."

He smiles at me, and there's an open innocence on his face. His eyes, for all his years of travelling are free of weight. How can that even be possible, I find myself wondering. It's clear that there's nothing silly to him about asking for friendship, or for offering it. I'm shocked by kind of wanting to hug him and cry. I have so much guilt, and I've tried so hard for so long not to think about what it means to watch all my friends die. And most of all for not wanting to go back home.

There's nothing I can do for him, and it's tearing me up.

How can Harry be so at ease?

"I'd like that," he says. "Reckon I have more stories."

"Cool," I say.

He smiles at me, and then he opens his front door, and turns back to me with a wink.

"Cool," he says.

And then, it's back to the airport.